Puck of the Starways

BY KEITH HILL

POETRY

The Ecstasy of Cabeza de Vaca
The Bhagavad Gita: A New Poetic Version
Interpretations of Desire:
Mystic Love Poems by the Sufi Master Ibn 'Arabi
I Cannot Live Without You:
Selected Poetry of Mirabai and Kabir
Psalms of Exile and Return
The Lounging Lizard Poet of the Floating World
Out of the Way World Here Comes Humanity!

FICTION

Blue Kisses
Interrogations: Selected Writing 1976 – 1990

NON-FICTION

The New Mysticism
The God Revolution
Striving To Be Human
Experimental Spirituality
Practical Spirituality
Psychological Spirituality
What Is Really Going On?
Where Do I Go When I Meditate?
How Did I End Up Here?

WITH PETER CALVERT

The Matapaua Conversations
The Kosmic Web
Learning Who You Are

Puck of the Starways

Keith Hill

Second edition published in 2022 by Disjunct Books
an imprint of Attar Books, New Zealand

Paperback ISBN 978-0-473-15993-1
Ebook ISBN 978-1-99-115706-5

Cover illustration by Rosie Colligan
Cover designed by Abigail Kerr

Disjunct Books is an imprint of Attar Books, a New Zealand publisher focused on spiritually oriented literature. For more information on Disjunct Books' publications visit:

www.attarbooks.com   www.keithhillauthor.com

Contents

Prologue

The sons and daughters of the Earth live in a wild and frightful world. It is a world of cataclysm and violence, of mystery and seeming unfathomableness, in which life is born painfully and all too suddenly curtailed. So it is now, and so it has been for ages since.

Yet life was not always so.

There once was a time when contentment and bliss animated all, when no shadows fell across any pleasures, and when all were satisfied and content.

So far was this era from the world humanity at present occupies that it was called the Land of the Happy. And a wonderful and extraordinary time it was, too.

Then magic wafted on the sunbeams. Then fairies played in the fields, and giants walked the Earth. In that time, humankind lived lives as frivolous and light as the breeze which skips over the flowers and sends their heads nodding gently from side to side.

They ate and drank with little thought of what they were or how they came to be. They were as ripples on the surface of the pond. And they sought no more.

But there was more. Much more.

For any world has within it another world, and is itself part of a larger world which embraces it from without. Just so, those living in the Land of the Happy had no conception of the world which resided in their own breasts. And, similarly, they did not know the greater world which encompassed them, of which they and their land formed an infinitesimal part.

Those in the Land of the Happy saw only the shimmering of the fields, and the towering of the mountains. Heard only the sighing of the wind, and the calling of the beasts. Felt only the warmth of the days, and the companionship of the night fire. Smelt only the fresh dawn rising out of the night mists, and the coolness of the gurgling streams. Tasted only the sweetness of their food, and the joy which coated all they did with honey.

What they experienced, they experienced truly. But their experience was limited. For never did they know the Gods who ruled their world. But those Gods knew them.

High above the Gods resided, beyond the tallest peak. To reach their abode a journey of vast distances was required, into the sky, past the Sun, and through a realm of galaxy upon galaxy, star-host upon star-host. This was the world of the Starways, the abode of the Gods.

Before the Earth was created, the Starways were ancient. And long after the Earth has vanished back into the Sun's fire the Starways will continue to administer over their allotted portion of creation. So the Inconceivable who created the All and Everything ordained it. And so it is still.

The Gods who occupied the Starways were intangible Gods. Unencumbered by bodies, they observed what they observed, and they did what they did. Mysterious are the ways of the Gods now, and mysterious were the ways of the Gods then.

But other beings inhabited the Starways, beings who were not themselves Gods, yet who lived in harmony with them, and whose presence was imbued with something of their mystery. Such a one of these lesser beings was Puck.

Day in and day out, never resting, Puck played. Having no body, he flitted from star to star, solar system to solar system. Ever at fun, he gambolled through the ten thousand veils of reality. Life to him was a joy, and that joy was his life's whole meaning.

However, when It created the All and the Everything, the Inconceivable also created the law of change. Nothing within creation escapes its consequences.

And so it was for Puck. He whose time-span was measured in units far exceeding an earthly aeon found that, in the end, he also could not escape time. And thus one day a message came to him from the very centre of the Starways. That message was a command.

"Puck, the Gods require you."

So away flew Puck. Away through the stars, away through clouds of solar systems wherein each system was as a speck of dust, and each speck hid ten million others. Faster than light he flashed through the Starways. And in a moment he was in the presence of the Gods.

The Gods of the Starways were awesome beings, existing far beyond the imagination's power to conceive of them. Their power resided in an intangible potency which, because formless, meant they could fill any part of the All and Everything with their dread presence. Yet they lived in hiddenness, apart.

Puck was a toy compared to their vastness. And a toy Puck felt as he stood in their midst. Sensing their profound power, he could not but tremble. So tremble he did.

And the Gods of the Starways spoke to Puck.

"Puck, your days of play have ended. Now you must enter into the activities of the Gods."

Puck bowed low and listened.

"Puck," said the Gods, "there is another world of which you know nothing. This world exists far from the Starways. It is called the Land of the Happy. By the decree of the Inconceivable, we Gods of the Starways administer over it. For many aeons the Land of the Happy has been true to its name. But everything changes. And now doubt and pain have entered the lives of those who dwell there. Go to the Land of the Happy, Puck. On behalf of the Gods, go and discover why this is so."

Puck bowed again before the overwhelming Gods.

And when he straightened, he discovered he was plunging away, out of the Starways, down through the ten thousand veils of reality, out of the regions of light, through the realms of time and space, into a different region altogether, of sights, sounds, and colours.

Ever faster he travelled, until a cacophony of impressions flooded him and, for a moment, he lost awareness of who, where or what he was.

The Three Wishes

When Puck returned to himself he found himself in a world very different from the Starways. Green fields stretched into the distance. Beyond them, forests of enormous and graceful trees rose high into an intense blue sky. And even further away stood the huge masses of mountains, their peaks sprinkled with snow.

Puck stood gazing at them for a long time, marvelling that such a world could exist. And as he did he came to realise that he *was* standing. Curious, he looked down at the body which surrounded him. And he smiled.

For, in sending him into the Land of the Happy, the Gods had given him the body of a youth whose limbs were filled with boundless energy. He stretched. He jumped. He ran.

But for only a short time. Because he was soon drawn to consider his task. Somewhere, somehow, doubt and pain had entered the Land of the Happy. And he was commanded to find it.

So away Puck went. Swift as the wind, as lightly as a leaf, Puck skipped over the grasses and began a reconnaissance. And, as he did, he gained his first view of the beings who lived in the Land of the Happy.

Small villages he passed, housing just a few people, several shouting children, one or two smiling elderly folk, a collection of goats and sheep. Through larger villages he flitted, wherein many families lived and worked contentedly together. By lonely outposts he sped, where only one or two existed in laughter and happiness.

And everywhere Puck went, he saw only satisfaction. Nowhere was there doubt, or despair, or pain. For these were the days before disease or famine, when work was small and not laborious, when the elements created no hardships, and when death came gently, as a wafting breeze in the night. Such was life to these people. They were as a ripple on the surface of a pond. And they sought no more.

As the days passed, then the weeks, Puck grew ever more skilful. Sometimes he took on the body of the beautiful youth which he had possessed when he first arrived. But at other times he became an elderly man, lame and prophetic, or a farmer who could read the clouds and air. Sometimes he became a woman, warm and maternal, and sometimes a bent grandmother who spat often and cursed small children for their noises, yet understood the secrets of herbs and plants.

Sometimes he even bypassed the human form altogether and became a crow flying high over humankind's heads. Or he changed into a deer which hovered tremulously at the edge of the forest, and when human beings approached leapt into the undergrowth.

Truly, Puck found a great satisfaction in all this. But his first joy was the little folk.

The little folk were delicate fairies, less than a human hand high, who he found playing on the fringe of a wood, where the trees gave way to grassed field, and sunlight filtered through the leaves, casting mottled shade and light on the ground.

Among these shadows the little folk made their fun. And what fun they had! Light as air, they floated on sunbeams, swung on flowers, catapulted from long grasses, hid behind leaves.

All this spontaneous playing reminded Puck of the Starways. So he immediately took on a fairy body and joined in. And being the generous creatures the little folk were, even though they knew he was not one of them, they gladly welcomed him into their game.

In and out of the shadows Puck darted, round the wild flowers, larking in the sunlight, letting his laughter tinkle with theirs up into the sky. Down he swooped onto another fairy, tumbling him onto the grass, then streaked away, chased by his new playmate.

On they both flew. Leaping from twigs. Hiding behind flowers. Dashing under gnarled tree roots. Plunging into bushes that tickled their feather-light bodies. However, without realising it their play soon led them away from the others, and they entered a less frequented part of the woods.

Puck looked around briefly, gaining his bearings. Then, to give his playmate a clue as to his whereabouts, he let out a shrill cry.

He was heard and, a second later, Puck's playmate tumbled off a dandelion and fell onto the grass beside him. Puck laughed.

Then, just as he was about to turn and fly on, he noticed the other fairy's face. The fairy was gazing fearfully at something past Puck's shoulder. Puck turned to see what had caused such unease. Observing, he smiled.

A man was attempting to hide behind a small bush, not far from the two fairies, his eyes wide with wonder.

Puck laughed. But his fellow fairy was not pleased. In a flutter of wings, he fled.

Puck made no move to follow. He wasn't afraid, for there

was nothing in the Land of the Happy that could harm him. Besides, he was interested to learn what this man would do. So he stood his ground and waited.

With a grunt, the man leaped out from behind the bush and made a clumsy attempt to grab Puck.

Puck considered. He easily could have escaped. But he wanted to discover what the man wanted. So he remained still.

Thick fingers closed around him as the man clasped Puck in both hands. Eyes alight, he jumped up and down.

"I've got one!" he shouted ecstatically. "I've got one!"

Puck sighed. "I would appreciate it if you didn't hold me so roughly," he said. "You'll injure my wings."

The man's fingers tightened as he leered at Puck.

"Oh no, you don't. I've caught you fair and square. Now you've got to give me my reward."

Puck raised a fairy eyebrow. "What reward?"

The man lifted Puck's body to eye-level and glared at him.

"You have to give me three wishes. Every time one of us catches one of you he gets three wishes. I claim mine right now. And I'm not letting you go until you give me them!"

Puck laughed.

But the man tightened his grip on Puck, peering at him through dangerous eyes.

"Don't muck me about," he growled. "I want my wishes."

Puck considered. Obviously, he did not have to give the man three wishes. On the other hand, the idea appealed to him. What would the man ask for? And what insight into these inhabitants of the Land of the Happy would be revealed? So he nodded.

"Agreed," he said. "But there are two conditions."

"What?"

"First, each of your wishes will last only from sunrise to

sunset. And second, whatever is done because of one wish cannot be undone by another."

"And you won't try to escape between times?"

Puck shook his head.

"We have a deal. But right now I've got a problem. How am I going to keep you hidden from everyone else? You see," the man licked his lips, "if the family sees you, they'll interfere and make me wish for something I don't want."

Puck's interest gathered. "I understand. I'll make myself invisible to everyone but you."

The man was astonished. "You can do that?"

"If I can grant you three wishes, I can perform the meagre trick of making myself invisible."

The man shrugged. "I was just asking."

And together they set off, the man loping in front, Puck flying invisibly behind.

Soon Puck found himself in a house full of joyfully shrieking children and bustling adults. The man, who had introduced himself as Waat, led Puck into a bedroom. There he opened a wooden box standing in the corner.

"Wait inside here," Waat said. "You'll be out of the way till bed time. I'll tell you my first wish then."

Laughing to himself, for he was enjoying this new situation immensely, Puck obeyed. The lid shut. And he waited.

Time passed. Household noises died away. Snores resounded through the house. Finally, as the rays of the moon died away, and the darkest period of night stood in the skies above the Land of the Happy, the box's lid opened and Puck flew out.

"Quiet!" Waat cautioned. "Everyone's asleep."

From the bed came the sound of Waat's wife breathing softly.

"What's your first wish?" Puck asked.

"I have heard stories of a dark place," Waat replied, "where strange and dangerous beings live. Some say that place burns with perpetual fires. Others claim its horrors are unimaginable. It's a place so terrible no one even dares to give it a name. Let me tell you, here and now, I, Waat, so dare. Magic fairy, I want to visit that place. And when I return from it to this world, I will be the one to give the unnameable a name. That is my first wish."

"Very well," Puck said. "When you next wake, you will be in that dark place that none dares name."

Satisfied, Waat replaced Puck in the box and closed the lid.

Morning came as usual in the Land of the Happy. The sky lightened, the sun rose, and human activity began. But, in the house of Waat, the day's start was less than perfect.

Waat woke to find himself in his usual bed, surrounded by his wife, children, and parents. He was perplexed. His magic fairy had obviously played a trick on him! Barely controlling his anger, he jerked open the lid of the box and glared down at Puck.

"What's happening here?" Waat hissed. "I thought I would be in the unnameable place today?"

Puck looked back at him placidly. "Wait," he commanded.

Waat's lip curled. Yet he had no choice but to accept Pucks' word. However, as he stamped around the house in search of breakfast, his temper became less amiable by the minute. Particularly the children annoyed him, running around the table, arguing over a slice of honey-coated bread.

"Stop it!" Watt screamed. "So help me, if you children don't stop I won't be responsible ... !"

This quietened the breakfast immediately. And the family sat at the table eating together as they always did at that hour. Soon all mouths were too occupied with eating to be worried about arguing, and comparative serenity reigned.

But only for a short while. Waat was visibly quivering with

repressed anger. Abruptly, he turned to his wife.

"Stop it," he screamed. "We've had enough!"

"What?" she asked, humouring him.

But Waat was in a shrieking frenzy. "For the sake of the gods and all that is good, enough!"

A ripple of agitation passed through the family.

"Got up on the wrong side of the bed this morning," muttered Waat's father, seated at the far end of the table.

Instantly, Waat stood and picked up a large chopping knife. He swung it in the direction of his uneasy family.

"Silence!" he roared.

Silence he immediately gained, except for the unpluggable crying of the youngest child. Waat's wife gathered the child to her breast. The older children quivered in their seats. Waat's elderly parents sat petrified in theirs.

Waat glowered at them all. Foam appeared on his lips, and his eyes glazed with rage. With a cry, he raised the knife over his head. Screams and pleas met the blade as he swung it down. To no avail. In an unnameable fit, he began slashing at all in the room.

Dusk found Waat sitting on the kitchen floor. Around him, chairs lay broken, tables were overturned over, and implements had been scattered across the room. The dead bodies of his family surrounded him. Dried blood ornamented everything. Waat sat in the midst of it all, uncomprehending.

Outside, the sun sank below the horizon. The edge of its burning disc vanished below, and the day's dying rays reached out across the Land of the Happy. Many villages and people it touched. And among them was Waat.

Waat emerged from his trance.

The first sight which met his eyes was that of Puck, standing before him in his fairy body. Then he looked around him.

Waat gasped. Tears welled in his eyes. He closed them in a desperate attempt to deny the reality around him. But when he reopened them, the horror remained.

"What happened? You great Gods above, what happened?" He looked pitifully at Puck. "Can you say? Who did this? Did those beings come up here from that dangerous place?"

Puck returned the gaze steadily. "You know you did this."

"B – but I – "

"What did you expect?" Puck responded. "Did you think that place none dare name was somewhere else?"

And Waat collapsed to the ground, weeping. Puck said no more. Full darkness descended. In its midst, Waat howled and groaned.

"I wish I could have them all back and safe again," he said in a dazed voice.

"That's not possible," Puck replied. "Surely, you remember the first condition? No wish can be used to undo the result of a previous wish."

Waat's groan became a prolonged howl. And Puck looked on compassionately. Finally, Waat collected his aching emotions. He beseeched Puck through tear-reddened eyes.

"Please, for tomorrow my wish is to be in heaven. I have heard it is a place of peace and beauty. After this, that is what I need. And I would like to see the souls of my poor family."

"It is done."

And they slept for the second night. The next morning shone bright and clear. Waat rose early. Again he was surprised.

"Is this heaven?" he asked Puck.

For he was still in his house. Frowning, he entered the kitchen. The bodies were there still, now covered with flies. An unkind aroma filled the room.

Puck stood in the air beside him. He merely smiled.

Waat, however, was making discoveries.

As the minutes passed, he felt a very peaceful state start to creep up onto him. Soon a feeling of love enthused him, so that everything in his sight was seen as good, and perfect, and complete. Even the bodies no longer adversely affected him. Lovingly, he took them outside, dug graves, and buried them. And he uttered a prayer over each body, thanking the Gods for their blessings.

In contrast to the previous day, now nothing upset him, and he remained in an even, peaceful temper. Waat felt good, and he experienced his life as good. Further, he now realized that everything that happened must conform to some secret plan of the Gods. A profound acceptance filled him, of what is, in the way it is.

Yet when the sun touched the horizon, and heaven died for him, Waat emerged from his loving state. Once again he was left feeling confused.

"I don't understand," Waat said. "I asked to go to heaven. But where were my family's souls? And where were the Gods?"

Puck smiled. "Clearly, heaven is not where you think. As for the Gods, they have never dwelled in heaven. Their abode is somewhere else altogether."

"Alright, then," Waat said decisively. "My third wish is to visit the abode of the Gods. The Gods command our lives. They decide what is and is not. I wish to visit them. And I will demand they take me to my family."

But Puck was shaking his head.

"Haven't you learned? Neither heaven nor the place that cannot be named were what you expected. Don't you consider it likely the abode of the Gods will differ from your expectations, too?"

Waat shrugged. He was long past thinking on such niceties.

"I've lost all I had. I'll take what comes."

"So be it," said Puck.

And they slept for a third night.

The next morning the sun's rays touched the roofs of the houses. All was not quite as usual, however. For when Waat awoke, he discovered that he had no body. Fear gripped him.

"What is happening?" his wordless cry asked.

Puck appeared beside him, similarly bodiless.

"You asked to visit the abode of the Gods," he answered. "The Gods have no bodies. To visit them, you must have no body, too."

That said, he led the way up from the Earth and towards the Sun. In a moment, they had flashed over the threshold, and were in the Starways.

Waat's wonder passed all bounds. Yet his fear was greater.

"Where are we?" he cried out.

"This is the Starways," Puck replied. "At the centre of the Starways are the Gods." He indicated the direction. "You must travel there alone. Go!"

And Puck vanished, leaving Waat in the Starways, uncertain and terrified. What should he do? But there was no alternative. It was happening as he had wished. He was being drawn towards the centre of the Starways.

Realising what was happening, his fear melted and a wave of exultation rose in him. At last, he thought, the secret plans of the Gods would be revealed. And he would be the very first among the sons and daughters of the Earth to question the Gods and learn their secrets.

And as he held onto this thought his fear ebbed away completely. Speeding towards the centre of the Starways, he foresaw the greatest of all possible results. So limited is humankind's vision. For as he sped towards through the Starways, Waat began to experience pressure. And the further he travelled, the stronger that pressure became. In fact, it was becoming distinctly stifling. Moreover, he was yet very distant from the Starways' centre.

Waat's exultation quickly returned to fear. He tried to slow his passage. He attempted to turn around. But he was powerless to alter his flight.

Instead, he was speeding up! Faster and ever faster, he flew.

Star clusters flashed past. Galaxies vanished in a moment. Nearer and ever nearer to the Starways' centre he travelled. But he was reaching the end of his capacities. For now the pressure around him had become truly crushing in its intensity.

Waat looked to where he was headed. The centre of the Starways was yet a great distance away. And still those pressures increased.

Terror filled Waat. He made one last attempt to stop. But it was too late. As a piece of flotsam is caught in a whirlpool, so he spun swifter and swifter towards the Starways' centre. Meanwhile, all around him, the enormous pressures grew.

Until, all too soon, the inevitable occurred.

The traveller was a puny being, and the Starways was a network of immense forces. The traveller was a being full of personal sentiments, and the Starways had only an impersonal existence. Where the powerful exist, the weak must give way. And this happened in the case of Waat. A mere speck in the galactic spaces, the tremendous presences in the Starways were too powerful.

Waat was crushed into nothingness. His consciousness was pulverised. He existed no more.

And such was his insignificance, that the Gods were oblivious to the fact that such a creature had dared to approach them at all.

You Shall Not Kill

The voice would brook no argument. The market this day was filled with jostling eager people and their manifold demanding clamouring and cries. Chickens squawked. Children stamped. Donkeys brayed. So the speaker was required to raise his voice to be heard.

"I say again. It is death to eat other creatures!"

Yet among all the market's exotic sounds, sights, and smells, the statement swirled away and was lost.

However, the speaker was not finished. He pointed a long, thin finger at the racks of meat arrayed on the table before him.

"You kill your own soul by eating those poor lambs!"

The speaker was a lanky, bearded man whose dress indicated a rustic origin, yet whose outward aspect was not without an element of command. He used this to full effect now, raising himself on his toes, bearing down on the jolly man whose stall lay before him, and speaking in a voice dripping with sarcasm.

"You realise that as godly beings we are not permitted to kill. Perhaps you consider you obey this law by murdering defenceless animals and eating them?"

The stall owner was unimpressed. "I work to feed my family. If I didn't, they would die. Wouldn't that be murder, too?

Now you're in the way of my customers. Yes, madam, how may I help you?" And the bearded man was pushed back by a crush of buyers.

However, this exchange had been observed by a swarthy, middle-aged farmer. Through his eyes looked Puck. Puck was impressed by the bearded man's intensity. He watched as the man walked away, muttering, through the market. Puck raised his hand.

And a spell was cast.

The enchanted man had soon left the village behind. He walked down a tree-lined track between cultivated fields. Presently, he departed from the track and strode over the slopes of a low hill.

Presently, he arrived at a stone cottage roofed with branches. In front of it a number of chickens pecked the smooth ground, and behind stood a vegetable garden full of sprouting corn, tomatoes, and beans. Of other people, there was no sign.

Inside, the man put down his market purchases and set about preparing a meal. From a safe he drew bread, butter, eggs, vegetables. Then he picked up a knife. Yet this action led to a strange occurrence. For the moment he lay the knife's blade on a tomato's skin, the tomato jumped out of the way!

The man looked at the knife. He looked at the tomato. He looked at his hands. And he shook his head, not believing what he had just seen. Setting his lips determinedly, he again grasped the tomato.

This time the tomato jumped as the knife was raised.

And the bearded man jumped, too!

He stood at the far side of the room, back against the wall, staring wide-eyed at the tomato on the table. It sat very still, behaving exactly as a tomato normally does.

Sweat suddenly stood in beads on the man's forehead. He

looked around the room. Everything appeared to be normal.

Water bubbled in the pot hanging over the hearth. The bed and two chairs were standing undisturbed in the corner. A breeze gently prodded the window's curtains. And his lunch was on the table, patiently waiting his attention.

He lowered his arms and made a concerted effort to shake himself out of his fright. Straightening his shoulders, he took one step towards the table. Towards the tomato. Nothing changed.

Regaining his confidence, he approached the table. In one quick motion, he picked up the tomato, placed it to one side, and stepped back. From a distance, he observed the tomato again. The tomato sat where he had placed it, not moving.

He sighed and allowed himself a tight smile. Apparently, he hadn't really seen what he thought he had. Relaxed now, he went back to the table, reached for the lettuce, and pulled off a leaf.

"Ouch!" said the lettuce.

The back of the man's head hit the wall behind him, so far did he jump. His mouth was open, his eyes stretched wide.

The lettuce sat on the table where he had dropped it.

"D-d-d-d-id you s-s-say something?" stammered the man.

"I certainly did," replied the lettuce. "You pulled off one of my leaves. How would you like me to pull off your finger?"

"B-but I was j-just preparing my lunch."

The lettuce rolled across the table to the tomato and put a sheltering leaf over it. "Sure. And what do you care if that means slicing up a poor tomato?"

"That's right," agreed the tomato. "It's as if he didn't know vegetables are alive."

And on the table the radishes, carrots, onions, and peppers rolled back and forth, muttering their agreement.

The man stared at them, appalled.

Yet, even as he stood there, he felt something strange gnawing at his back. Uneasily, he glanced over his shoulder.

The flowers in the pot on the window-sill had all turned to face him. The leaves of the ivy outside were pressed up hard against the glass and were rubbing against it, squeaking vociferously. Even the weeds had leaned in through the open doorway. He shivered under their penetrating glare.

For a full minute the man looked from one vegetable to the next, feeling their tiny glares eating into him. Then he cracked.

He turned, ran through the open doorway, and raced howling out of the cottage, across the grass.

"Eeee!" "Ooh!" "Eaow!" screamed the blades of grass as his pounding feet mashed them into the hard ground.

He pulled up and looked back. The vegetables inside the cottage were shrieking. The vegetables in the garden moaned. The grass under his feet writhed. And the man howled.

Followed by a cacophony of voices, he ran over the hill behind the cottage, and disappeared from sight.

The sun sank. The sun rose.

Morning nudged its warm light through the cottage windows, falling across the table. All had returned to normal.

The vegetables lay where they had been left. The flowers in the pot were standing naturally. The ivy at the window faced its leaves out from the cottage wall, absorbing the sun's warm light.

Around the cottage, it was life as usual. Near the whitewashed walls chickens fought over a worm. Further away, an untethered goat pulled at the grass. However, no voices were audible, no shrieks.

The only sound was the wind blowing the corn in the garden, and the creaking of the open cottage door. Of the bearded man, there was no sign. Not here, that is. Yet he was not far away.

Just over the hill behind the cottage, from the branch of a tree, twine around his neck, the bearded man hung. The wind tugged at his shirt and ruffled his hair. But he neither felt it nor moved. He was dead.

The sun sank. The moon rose.

The moon sank. The sun rose.

Bitten by ants, pecked by birds, blown by flies, buffeted by the sun, wind, and rain, the corpse swung to and fro. And, presently, life replaced death. Its skin began to crawl.

Under the skin's surface, emerging from thousands of tiny eggs, larvae began to hatch. Warmed by the sun, probing, burrowing and excavating, they fed on the ripening flesh. Soon fat worms crawled from the corpse's nostrils, from its mouth, from the yellowed eruptions on its face and arms.

And one among those feasting worms wore the grinning face of Puck.

The Man Who Would Be Wise

The seasons passed. Further adventures presented themselves to Puck. But through them all he did not forget the task the Gods had given him. Somewhere, someone in the Land of the Happy was sad. And it was Puck's challenge to find who this person was.

When night fell, the inhabitants of the Land of the Happy slept. But not Puck. Conscious of his burden, he flew far and wide, to the four corners of the land, in search of that one who was sad.

And so it was that, one day, Puck heard talk of one who was sad and who lived by himself on the edge of the ocean. It was a passing wonder among the people. A man who could be sad in the Land of the Happy, they observed. How could that be? Yet this was just another wonder among many.

For there was the wonder of the sun rising each day. And the wonder of the birds which danced and swooped through the air. And the wonder of the world around them which grew so colourful and lovely. And it passed among these other wonders, and was lost. But not to Puck.

Swifter than the breeze which runs and tumbles, head over heels, across the tops of the trees, he flashed to the edge of the ocean. And there he found that one in the Land of the Happy who was sad.

The man was seated on a rock on the beach, looking out over the waves, which beat one after the other, endlessly, on the shore. His eyes were the most mournful Puck had yet seen in his adventures in the Land of the Happy.

Puck stepped towards him.

"Hello," Puck said. "I've come a very long way to see you."

The man should have been startled. But he was so numbed that he did not even look up. Instead he shrugged and kept his eyes on the waves.

"You are unique," Puck said. "You are sad when everyone else is happy. Why is that?"

Still the man remained silent.

"I will not leave until you answer."

The waves continued to lap onto the shore. At last, the man opened his mouth and replied.

"I am sad," he said, "because I am not wise."

Puck was astonished. That is, he was as astonished as a being from the Starways could be.

"What do you mean, you are not wise?"

The man picked up a piece of wood and threw it onto the water. Together, they watched it bob on the waves.

"We are like that driftwood. We float on the surface of life, never able to glimpse the depths. But I wish to see those depths. That is what I mean when I say I am not wise. And because I know I shall never see them, I have become sad."

"How can you say that?" Puck objected. "Look around you. See what a wonderful world you live in. The breeze is blowing, the waves are lapping, the sea-birds are calling, the sand is warm. You have food and shelter. You have all you need. How can this not be sufficient for you and your kind?"

Finally, the man looked up.

"All that is true," he said sharply. "This world is happy. And we are alive. Yet we are ignorant. People say we are ruled by the Gods. Perhaps this is true. But I don't see them. Where are they? Do we live in their light? Or is this land the crumbs they left behind when they departed? It is cruel for the Gods to keep us in ignorance. Either let us be wise as they must be. Or let death stamp on us and end our existence forever. For I cannot endure this situation even one day longer."

Puck was enjoying this conversation immensely. "Surely you don't wish to die before your time!"

"If I remain ignorant, it makes no difference whether I die today, or tomorrow, or a thousand years hence. In the end it is all the same. Emptiness and nothing."

And with that the man closed his eyes, lowered his head onto his arms, and would speak no more.

Ten thousand thoughts raced through Puck's mind. Could it be as it appeared? Could this man really crave wisdom? Is wisdom even something human beings might be capable of possessing?

Puck knew what he needed to do. So he called out the secret name of the Gods.

Immediately, he felt himself being lifted out of his body, into the skies, then pulled past the Sun, through the hidden doorway, and back into the world which is the Starways. Once again, great presences surrounded the diminutive Puck. Once again, he bowed low before the Gods.

"Puck," commanded the Gods, "report your findings."

"I went to the Land of the Happy," he said. "I found the one there who is sad. And I discovered the reason for his sadness."

"And what is his reason?" asked the Gods.

"The man is sad," Puck responded, "because he is not wise."

And around him Puck felt the Gods rejoicing. Their titanic laughter shook the Starways. Their satisfaction redounded through the ten thousand veils of reality. Their tears watered a million worlds. And Puck stood in their midst, and wondered.

"Puck," said the Gods when they had completed their rejoicing, "we have waited aeon after aeon for one from the Land of the Happy to say what you have just told us. We are elated. For when the Inconceivable created the All and the Everything, It hid wisdom in a special place. It buried that place deep within the ten thousand veils of reality. And It proclaimed that nothing of value should be easily obtained. Accordingly, only those who search and struggle will find wisdom. But there will be frustration, too. And emptiness and pain of lack. And even, at times, suffering. So return to the Land of the Happy, Puck. Return and tell that one who is sad that if he wants wisdom for himself and for his people, the price to be paid is struggle, frustration, emptiness, pain, and suffering."

Away flashed Puck. And in a trice he found himself back on the shore, standing in front of the man who was sad.

But this time the man was standing too, an astonished expression on his face. For he had seen Puck appear from out of the air. And that meant he was in the company of one who was not of this world. He threw himself on his knees.

"Forgive me! How could I know you were of the Gods."

Puck smiled.

"I am merely a messenger of the Gods. They have replied to your complaint that you lack wisdom. Know that they are pleased with your sentiment. But there is a price to be paid for the acquisition of wisdom. For only those who struggle can achieve wisdom."

The man was ecstatic. "I can see there must be a price. I am more than content with what you say."

"There is more," Puck stated. "The price may be struggle. But struggle does not walk alone. In its shadow slides a feeling of lack. And when lack arrives, so does discontent. Discontent has a cousin, frustration. And where discontent and frustration hold hands, emptiness reigns. Know emptiness carries the knife of suffering. And that knife penetrates the heart. All this means an irreversible change to your existence. Think well on this before you respond."

But the man could scarcely contain his excitement.

"I understand what you are saying," he said. "It is natural that wisdom should have such a price, and that our existence will change irrevocably. But I am content if the Gods have proclaimed that it must be so."

"The price of wisdom," Puck continued, "is that you and all your fellow beings will no longer live in the Land of Happy. Your world will become a land of doubt and heartache and anguish. Unhappiness and pain and misery will stalk you all. And emptiness will fill you. Think it over well. Is this truly what you desire?"

"I don't need to think on that," the man said. "Life which is not always happy, which is difficult and hard, yet which contains a purpose, is incomparably better than a life which is easy, yet leads nowhere, and which does not see into the way of things. I accept the will of the Gods. I kneel and assent to their decree."

And with that the man fell silent. Truly, this was a moment befitting silence. So Puck sat beside him and spoke no more.

But when the sun sank, and the stars came out, and the moon rose, and all in the Land of the Happy soundly slept, Puck called out the secret name of the Gods. And in a moment found himself again in their presence.

"Well, Puck," demanded the Gods, "what is your report?"

"I visited the Land of the Happy," Puck said. "I spoke to the one there who is sad. And I told him the price of wisdom."

"That is well done," said the Gods. "What is his reply?"

"His reply," said Puck, "is that if feelings of dissatisfaction, lack, frustration and suffering are the price of wisdom, he and his kind are satisfied to pay it."

And again the Gods rejoiced. Again their pleasure echoed through the Starways. Again their tears washed ten million worlds. And the God's made their proclamation.

"We Gods are not spiteful Gods. We carry out only what the Inconceivable has ordained. And It has ordained that the sons and daughters of the Earth must do as they shall do, and be as they shall be, in order to become wise. Yet when they are wise, they will take their places among us. And we will share our duties with them joyfully, for that is what the Inconceivable decreed when It created the All and the Everything. So go now, Puck. Return to the Land of the Happy. Return to the sons and daughters of the Earth and help them as you are able. Surely, they will need your aid and guidance, and all our collective love and compassion. For that is as the Inconceivable has arranged their existence. Now go."

Puck bowed.

Then down he flew, down to the Land of the Happy. But when he reached there, he saw it was the Land of the Happy no more. For the Gods of the Starways had spoken truly. They had done what the Inconceivable decreed they should do.

They had removed contentment. They had withdrawn happiness. They had ended whatever satisfaction the Earth's sons and daughters had previously felt with what floated on life's surface. And they had replaced it with a longing for something more.

Now shadows strode across the Land of the Happy. Now,

all was not peaceful. All was no longer harmonious. Broils broke out. Fights and wars. Diseases ate holes in bodies. And sickness and despair attacked all without distinction.

Now death stalked in daylight. And he no longer took people gently. Instead, he wielded a scythe. And where he plundered, there was an aftermath of lamentation. Where before people had laughed without thinking, now they tried not to think. And when they did think, they wept.

And the Gods created the villages of Er and Orr. And they filled the Sea of Desolation with the madness of the Moon. And from the Moon's shadow they created the Mountains of What Cannot Be. And on one side of those Mountains they shaped the Valley of the Never Was. While on the far side they laid out the Desert Plain.

And in the middle of the Desert Plain they sat Sorrow, who wept day and night, without cessation. And from Sorrow's tears they formed a river.

And that river they directed to flow through the vales which suckled all those who lived in the Land of the Happy. And whoever drank of that river went mad. And there was none alive who, at some time in his or her life, did not drink thereof.

Yet the Gods were not malicious in their intent. They wished only the best for all charges. And to show their compassion, they left sparkles of sunlight in that shadowy world, as reminders of what could be experienced when humankind achieved wisdom. So none suffered all the time, but rather experienced flashes of happiness which briefly illuminated their lives. Those flashes may have been infrequent. Yet they were passionately remembered, and were clung to long after they had passed.

Pinched by lack, battered by despair, some viewed those flashes as a divine joke, given by the Gods that the sons and daughters of the Earth might suffer the more. Yet in others, who experienced dissatisfaction, emptiness, discontent, and lack, there gradually developed an understanding that the Gods were kind in doing so. And they took those flashes as they were meant, as gifts to be used for celebration.

And this was how the Land of the Happy was transformed into to the Land of the Sad.

Yet all were not sorrowful in that altered world. For that one who had asked the Gods to act so was far from discontent. In the Land of the Sad, there was now one who was happy. Such irony was not lost on those who observed it.

And such irony has accompanied the sons and daughters of the Earth ever since.

The Villages of Er and Orr

Puck revelled in his new role of caring for his charges. Day and night, tirelessly, he flew over hills, across meadows, around villages. And thus it was that one day he came upon the villages of Er and Orr.

The villages of Er and Orr were situated on either side of a small volcanic mountain range, separated by a bleak ridge, the top of which was a smoking, lava-filled crater.

Fortunately, in the many years the villages had been there, this crater had never done more than belch gases and smoke. Much more dangerous was the great forest which surrounded the mountain range, and that grew right up to the outskirts of each village, pinning them against the volcano's foothills.

This forest was called the Brooding Dark. Rumour maintained a terrible giant, Ton-gu, walked its paths. Ton-gu had one hundred heads, an enormous hairy body, and carried a giant sword in one massive hand. Beyond all doubt, those who inhabited the Land of Sad considered this giant to be the most fearsome, most dangerous, most merciless monster in the whole world.

People who lived on the fringes of the Brooding Dark told stories of how whispers would slither through the trees, then fall on lone travellers from above. Coiling around their victim's neck, the whispers would tighten around that unfortunate until he or she was securely bound and could no longer move. Then tiny monsters would attack, filthy hobgoblins, and small toad-like creatures, whistling from burrows, rustling in the under-growth, shrieking through the tree-tops, until the trapped traveller was utterly frozen with fear.

Finally, Ton-gu arrived. Each of its one hundred heads would be whispering, and each of those whispers would torment the trapped victim even further, until he was so terrified he craved his own death. Then Ton-gu struck. With its sword it cut the poor victim into one hundred pieces and fed its one hundred mouths one piece each. Then, its appetite momentarily appeased, Ton-gu strode off in search of new fools to torment, new victims to devour.

All this the peoples of Er and Orr well knew. And they prided themselves on their ability to escape the wiles of Ton-gu. No meal of rapacious fools they. No, they were knowing peoples, intimate with the dangers of their world.

Lesser peoples might have worshipped Ton-gu, making offerings to ensure it remained within the confines of the Brooding Dark, and never entered their villages in search of victims. But they, in their wisdom, were above such primitiveness. And so they eschewed Ton-gu and worshipped the Gods. And their lives were as they choose them to be.

All this Puck in a short time discovered and understood. But as he watched from the ridge separating the two villages, he could discern a fear set deep in those villagers' hearts. And he resolved to discover what it might be.

The afternoon was warm. Wearing the body of a wild cat, Puck padded down from the ridge, towards the village of Er. He paused at the corpse of a deer which had fallen from a cliff above, to gnaw the flesh and to lick, with a coarse tongue, the sweet marrow leaking from its shattered bones. Then on he padded. A few minutes later, he came across a villager sleeping in the shade cast by an ancient tree.

Apparently, the villager had been gathering berries and nuts, because a bag lying on the ground beside him bulged with them. But this is not what drew Puck's attention. For as he slept, the man's face jumped and jerked.

Intrigued, Puck padded over and sniffed him with a feline snout. The villager was dreaming. But what? Puck determined to find out.

He silently uttered the secret name of the gods. And the wild cat vanished from sight, to be replaced by ... nothing!

Yet Puck was not a nothing. He had become a thought, and on the insubstantial back of that thought he rode deep inside the sleeping villager's mind.

To his surprise, Puck found himself in a world exactly the same as Er and its surrounding environs. The same rocky foothills. The same cultivated fields. The same Brooding Dark, intense with dankness and fear. Indeed, as Puck looked around, he recognised the very tree under which his sleeper now lay dreaming.

Yet there was one important difference. For in his dream the villager was not asleep. He was awake. Moreover, the villager was running!

Gasping, panting, the villager ran as fast as he could over the rocks. Yet, despite his efforts, he was making little progress. And he realised it, for his fear visibly grew with every step. But from what was he running? The giant, Ton-gu, with its one hundred slobbering heads? Or something even worse? Some nightmare so terrible it lacked even a ghostly resemblance to human form?

As if in answer to this question, the villager glanced over his shoulder, eyes wide with panic.

Puck followed his eye-line. In thought he searched the rocks and crevasses behind the villager, inspecting each cranny and cave. And he saw nothing. The frightened villager was running in terror from nothing!

At that moment, the villager stopped in his tracks. His head jerked upwards. High above, on a rocky ledge, three men were visible. The villager stared, horrified, as a huge boulder dislodged by the men fell, crashing and bouncing, straight towards the villager. With a cry, the sleeping villager woke.

He sat up. His breath jerked convulsively. His limbs shook. Perspiration ran down his temples and had soaked his shirt. Then he heard it. The sound of stone on stone.

He looked around. At the trees. At the rocks. At the cliff-face. Nothing stirred. That left only above. His eyes jerked upwards.

High above a rock was falling, striking the jagged ledges of the cliff-face as it bounced and crunched its way down.

The villager jumped to his feet. A second later the rock crashed into the ground where he had been sleeping, and shattered into a thousand pieces!

The villager froze, amazed he was still alive. Yet as he did so, his eyes wandered up the cliff-face which towered above him, seeking the boulder's source.

High above, so far away they were barely visible, three men could be seen. And just below them, threatening to be loosed by their activity, was still another boulder, of even more massive dimensions, ready to crush him into oblivion. With a scream, the villager took to his heels, and was gone.

Puck smiled ruefully to himself. But only for a moment. Because in the next he was soaring on the wings of an owl, up towards the mountain ledge from which the boulder had come. Did those above deliberately dislodge the boulder in an attempt to kill the villager from Er? He soon had his answer. For he discovered that one of the three men above had slipped while walking the mountain path.

He hung over the ledge, his legs wildly groping for leverage, held only by his two frantic companions. And he was slipping from their grasp. A sleeve tore, and the dangling man slipped further.

All three men cried out.

Puck considered. Should he intervene? However, before he could decide, the two shouted in unison. Making a huge effort, they pulled their companion back on to the path.

Puck's heart sang with theirs as he watched them embrace each other, hug the earth, and shout their thanks to the Gods.

Soon, gliding on the air currents, Puck watched as they made their excited way along the ridge and around the smoking volcanic crater. Far below the ridge, in a lush valley, lay the thatched roofs of the village called Orr. Seeing their homes, the three quickened their steps.

Soon they were sharing news of their good fortune. Then, kneeling in the village square, they offered up a prayer of gratitude. And their fellow villagers knelt with them as they praised all the benevolent Gods.

Night fell.

In both Orr and Er, food was cooked and eaten. But the moods in each village were quite different. For where Orr's inhabitants were in a celebratory mood, those of Er were hunched over their fires, backs stiff, lips rigid. From a tree in the centre of Er, an owl containing Puck watched.

The villager Puck had seen earlier was angry. And he was telling how three from Orr had attempted to kill him!

"They've hated us for years," came the hissed response.

"So of course that's what they tried to do."

"Praise be to the Gods they didn't succeed."

"But if we don't act now, next time they will."

"They're animals."

"Only revenge can pay them back for this!"

"Death to all those from Orr!"

And with some ancient enmity feeding their thoughts, they muttered exactly what revenges they would carry out. Long into the night they swore, argued, and connived. And only when they were all agreed on the details of what they would do the following morning did they cease their maledictions and go to bed.

Yet the villagers' rage was not the only stirring that night. There was restlessness, too, deep within the Brooding Dark. In all the long years Ton-gu had stalked the forest paths, it had never once left those dank trees and entered the villages of Er and Orr. But this night that changed.

Because as the villagers of Er entered their warm hovels, closed their eyes, and drifted off to sleep, deep in the forest the giant awoke. Its two hundred eyes jerked open. As one, its one hundred noses sniffed the air. Together those eager noses wrinkled. Simultaneously, those keen eyes narrowed. For on the cool night air wafted the moist, delicious smell of blood.

Wide awake now, Ton-gu unfolded its curled limbs, heaved its giant body into activity, and stepped out of its lair. The scent of blood was heavy in the cool night air.

Ton-gu paused only long enough to sniff from what direction that scent came. Then it set its great thighs into motion, and crashed off through the undergrowth, into the darkness.

Shortly, Ton-gu was standing on the edge of Er.

Outwardly, the village looked peaceful. Its square was deserted, its hovels silent, its inhabitants softly snoring. Only the glowing embers of a few fires provided any sign of life.

Yet peace has an inward as well as an outward component. And inwardly Er was not as peaceful as it appeared to be. For, emanating from the villager's heads, rising through their hovels' roofs, hovering just above their dry thatch, were the villager's dreams. And through these dreams unrestrained acts of blood-letting stamped. It was these dreams that had generated the blood-filled scent to which Ton-gu was now drawn.

Ton-gu's one hundred noses twitched. Its two hundred eyes gleamed. Never before had this happened in the histories of Er and Orr. But just because it hadn't occurred before, didn't mean it could not occur now.

Its eyes increasingly glazed, Ton-gu stalked between Er's hovels, sniffing the villagers' fevered dreams. Aware of the giant's presence, a mongrel whined. Ton-gu stamped once, and it whined no more.

Ton-gu took its time, savouring the scents, enjoying the chance to choose which to pursue.

Until finally, outside a large hut, it paused. Here the hovering dream was fat with severed limbs and exploded guts. The lips of one hundred drooling mouths smiled. Ton-gu's huge arms reached through the doorway below him, fumbled around inside, and pulled out an old man, so terrified he could not whimper, let alone shout to his fellow villagers to save him. Strong hands dangled him before a hundred snapping mouths. He fainted. And in a trice Ton-gu and his victim were gone.

Morning saw day-lit pandemonium replace Er's noxious midnight dreams. If the oaths and promises of the preceding night had been violent, the disappearance of one of their own meant only death would be sufficient punishment for those responsible.

"And we all know who is to blame!" shrieked the family of the one who had been taken.

"Those swine from Orr!" came the collective response.

It was resolved. Revenge would be exacted that very day.

Cheers, jeers, and prophecies accompanied the four chosen executioners as they made their way out of the village and up the mountain path which led to Orr. Revenge did not prove to be at all time-consuming.

No sooner had the would-be executioners reached the crater smoking on the ridge above the village, than they came across the very circumstance they so passionately desired. A lone villager from Orr was chipping crystals from rock near the crater's edge.

Engrossed in her task, she did not notice the four approaching her. With a triumphant cry they picked her up, carried her screaming, kicking body to the crater's edge, and threw her into the boiling mud below. She disappeared with a soft plop.

Soon, the four were trading stories and slapping backs as they made their laughing way to Er. And that night, a people so recently mournful celebrated their evening meal with wine and song.

Meanwhile, Orr was lost in lamentation. The dead woman's pick had been discovered at the crater's lip, along with a shoe. The footprints of four men were visible, along with signs of a struggle. Only one group could be responsible.

"Those murderers from Er!" came the cry.

"Last year our vines withered."

"And six of my goats died."

"That was all due to their witchccaft."

"Now we must return to them what their acts of darkness demand!"

And that night they sat up long past the time the logs had

burned down and been replenished, as they invented punishments and revenges sufficiently horrible to repay those who had, throughout the years, so viciously harried and persecuted them. Only when revenges had been planned, and executioners were assigned, did they retire to their beds and allow smiles to accompany their bloodied drift towards sleep. Yet as their eyes closed, and their racing thoughts slowed, and sleep took them into the realm of fevered dreams, on Orr's outskirts dry twigs cracked.

For Ton-gu had smelt the blood in their thoughts. And now, its massive lips dribbling saliva, the giant stood in the darkness, watching savage dreams blossom above the villagers' thatched roofs.

And for the first time Ton-gu entered Orr. And for the first time its immense arm groped around inside one of its huts. And for the first time Orr suffered the loss of one of its own to the giant and its hundred ravenous mouths. Little did the villagers of Orr realise what would assuredly follow when they woke the next morning and howled at the disappearance.

But Puck foresaw very clearly indeed.

Two hours later, when six armed men from Orr climbed the mountain path to exact retribution from those of Er, a group from Er had anticipated them, and lay in wait on the ridge above. Screamed confrontation was quickly followed by the thud of clubs.

And in both villages that night voices made lamentation.

Thereafter neither village knew a peaceful night's sleep. Fear, suspicion and dread ever stalked through their thoughts. No one went out alone. All trembled at the least and most innocent of sounds, terrified lest they should be the next to die.

And through it all Ton-gu prospered. Called by the villagers' bloodthirsty dreams, Ton-gu regularly visited both Er and

Orr, carrying off in the darkness bodies on which to feast. For which disappearances, Er blamed Orr, and Orr blamed Er. And Ton-gu grew fatter and ever more insatiable.

Puck witnessed it all. The bloodshed. The violence. The despair. Until, finally, he decided that was enough. Compassion compelled him to intercede.

Dusk was falling as an elderly, bent man limped into the village of Er. He ambled into the village centre, feeling the power of the villagers' cold and suspicious stares.

"Who are you?" a mother called out as she gathered her two children to her skirts.

"Are you sure you're not from Orr?" cried another, half hidden in a doorway.

"Can't be," responded a third from behind a window. "Far too good looking."

The old man halted in the middle of the village square.

"Call everyone in," he croaked. "I have important news."

It took very little time, because the villagers of Er had ceased tending the fields or gathering food from the mountainside. And, besides, they were far fewer than they had been a month before.

Soon, they were standing around the old man, scrutinizing him balefully. Puck cleared his wrinkled throat.

"I am come today from the temples of Wa-Zu, to convey to you a message from the Gods."

A sigh rose from the gathered crowd, followed by muttered exchanges. None had heard of such a temple before. But with such a name it could only be very important. Pleased with having engaged their attention so easily, Puck spoke.

"By the authority of the Wa-Zu priests' visions, and by their insight into the Gods' mysterious will, I am here to inform you of how you came to be in this unhappy situation."

And he recounted the events of the past few weeks, starting with the villager's dream of being chased, and the misinterpreted falling boulder. Puck described Ton-gu's first midnight foray into Er, then how the giant had entered Orr. He detailed how now neither Er nor Orr originally attacked one another, but that Ton-gu had strode among them at night, carrying off whom it desired, making both villages its helpless and weeping victims.

Wonder filled the square. Could this be true? Could it be that only Tun-gu's actions were keeping the animosities between Er and Orr stoked? At first, some thought it might well be so. But soon a stumbling block to the story was offered.

"Has any here ever seen the giant near here?"

"Has any sign been found that it has been in our village?"

"Of course not!"

And discussion raged long into the night.

Finally the village elder stood, called for silence, and pronounced the villagers' judgement.

"Emissary from Wa-Zu, we appreciate your risking the dangers of the Brooding Dark to visit us here and tell us of the priests' glorious visions. We acknowledge the wisdom of others should never be lightly rejected."

But now the elder's voice hardened.

"However, we of Er are not empty of wisdom ourselves. For years we have known how close the giant Ton-gu lived to us. Yet never have we worshipped it. Never have we offered it appeasement or sacrifice. Such a people as us the Gods reward, not torment. Certainly they would not send a giant to devour us."

A murmur of assent rose from the assembled villagers.

"Emissary, the visions of the priests of Wa-Zu are appreciated. But they are wrong. Only Orr is responsible for those who have been taken from us. No one and no thing else can be blamed."

Puck was a being from the Starways, and privy to ten thousand mysteries. Yet the human heart was a labyrinth in which even one of his experience could lose his way. So the cheers approving the elder's words that accompanied Puck as he left the village caused a great wonder to rise in his heart. It was a wonder that caused him to consider the limitations on what he might achieve with these people. Nonetheless, that night Puck decided he must try again.

Early the next morning, the same elderly man limped into Orr. As he had the previous day, he made his way to the village square. Warily, the villagers gathered around him. By degrees, their voices stilled. And Puck spoke.

"People of Orr, I come from the priests of Wa-Zu with a message from the Gods."

As in Er, a sigh of wonder rose from those gathered. As in Er, they were flattered the Gods considered them sufficiently important to be sent a communication. As in Er, Puck said what compassion compelled him to say.

He described how the giant Ton-gu was responsible for the majority of Orr's deaths, and how it was Orr's own fevered thoughts and dreams which kept attracting Ton-gu back to the village. He concluded by stating that to stop Ton-gu from entering Orr, the villagers must stop dreaming of bloody revenge.

A babble of voices met this solution to their troubles. Many and loud were the arguments which followed. Finally, the village elder stamped his staff on the hard-packed earth, and made his reply.

"Messenger from the priests of Wa-Zu, we appreciate your words. I can see that what you say is sincerely felt. But you are wrong. We of Orr have never offered Ton-gu blood worship. And neither do we today. Assuredly, only Er is responsible for our misery. People of Orr, know no one else is our enemy. None else can be blamed!"

Puck left with the agreeing cheers of Orr ringing in his ears. He had tried. But now the only course left for him was to sit back and watch. So watch he did.

Dawn found the remnants of both villages bowed in prayer.

"You Gods above," cried the elder of Er, "you only do we worship. You only do we love. Give us the reward such loyalty deserves. Destroy our enemies. Reduce them to dust. For in being enemies to us, they assuredly prove themselves also enemies to you."

Meanwhile in Orr, kneeling amidst the rising smoke of incense, the village elder solemnly intoned a similar prayer.

"You great Gods, hear your loyal worshippers' pleas. Today our enemies harry us. We ask only that you punish them with what they perversely wish on us."

Above the smoking volcano's crater, the owl that was Puck glided and listened.

"Gods, accept our supplications."

"Reward those who think only of you."

"Punish those who would punish us."

"Hound, curse, and torment them!"

"Disturb, harass, and kill!"

But not only Puck was listening. And other eyes besides Puck's watched. Thousands of eyes. Each one screaming with hunger. For throughout the weeks of enmity, Ton-gu had been so well fed that it had given birth. Not to a single child. To a brood.

And now, attracted by the bloody thoughts of those knelt in prayer, a dozen ravenous giants stood outside each village. Their thousands of eyes rolled. Their hundreds of mouths drooled. Their numerous swords were raised, ready to cut and swath. This brood was too large not to be observed.

Simultaneously, in both Er and Orr, Ton-gu was seen. A double horror-filled cry went up.

"The giant is here!"

"A brood of giants!"

"Run!"

But they were too late.

The giants were already chopping, mangling, and crushing. Immediately, prayers changed to cries of anguish.

"Emissary, tell the priests of Wa-Zu we believe their visions!"

But Ton-gu's brood was loosed now, and events could not but run their course. The hungry horde of giants tore limbs, chewed bones, lapped hot brains from shattered skulls, and tongued the marrow from shattered bones.

Seeing all was lost, Er's elder pulled himself out of a giant's grip, and managed to utter a last, tremendous plea. "You great Gods above, do whatever you will. But destroy this evil brood!"

And in Orr the same cry was uttered. "You Gods, do what we must to save us from this terror!"

The Gods of the Starways are compassionate. They hear what they hear, and they do what they do. Even though they existed far from the Land of the Sad, they felt echoes of the pain felt by the the villagers of Orr and Er. So they caused a response to the villagers' cries for help.

The volcano above both villages exploded. With a single, violent heave, rocks and lava spewed high unto the air, then rained on the shrieking villagers below.

Ton-gu and his brood expired in an instant. As did all those still alive in the villages of Er and Orr.

Shortly, an owl sailed overhead, its sharp eyes examining the scene below.

There was no movement. Not a granary, not a house, not a

roof, not a stick stood. Nothing indicating any human presence at all stuck out from the piles of jagged rocks and glowing lava.

The owl circled each violated village once. It then flapped its wings, lifted over the Brooding Dark, and vanished from sight.

At the Top of the World

*P*uck stood at the foot of a towering mountain range, staring up at the snow-draped peaks poking into the clear blue sky. A chill wind blew off the peaks and wrapped around his body, telling him what the sensation of being alive meant in the Land of the Sad.

As Puck stood there, enjoying the chilled air, he became aware of a cloud of dust rising from the road behind him. The cloud was caused by a man riding a horse. They were moving very fast.

Puck waited.

A few minutes later the rider and his mount arrived.

Seeing Puck seated on the roadside, he reigned in his sweating horse and looked down.

"Hello stranger," called the horseman.

"Hello, traveller," replied Puck.

"Going up the mountain?"

"I am. What about you?"

The horseman glanced up the trail. He nodded. "I expect you've heard the rumours."

"No."

"They say there's a sniper at the top of the pass who kills any who dare travel through it."

"You don't sound convinced."

"Rumours are the product of scared men thinking too much by the night fire."

And with that he whipped his horse, it reared, and they galloped up the trail.

Puck watched the two disappear round a bend in the trail. Then he threw away his staff and, gathering his cloak around him, whirled on the spot.

The body of the young adventurer vanished, replaced by a crow flapping the air. The crow hovered a moment, then heaved its wings and began climbing.

Riding the air currents, it rose up the mountainside. Up he flew, feeling the air currents as they whirled over his wings, ruffling his feathers, buffeting him from side to side. The exhilaration was thrilling.

Presently, Puck neared a peak overlooking the pass which wound its jagged way through outcrops of rocks, clumps of hardy tussock grass, and shrunken shrubs.

On either side of the pass ravines yawned dangerously, while at numerous points cliffs fell away altogether, dropping into chasms thousands of feet deep.

Puck swooped on the air currents, looking for the sniper. He soon found him.

The sniper was huddled at a strategic point overlooking the pass. Boulders hid him from the view of anyone coming up, but he could see down without obstruction. In the crook of his arm nestled a crossbow.

Puck settled on a small ledge sheltered from the wind. With a clear view of both the sniper and the pass, he waited.

Shortly, the sound of a horse's hooves crunching small

stones could be heard. Then the harsh voice of the rider urging on his mount.

The sniper straightened. The wind ruffling his shaggy beard, he raised the crossbow to his shoulder.

As if deliberately daring danger, the horseman sang stoutly as he rode into the view.

The sniper drew up his crossbow.

He aimed.

He squeezed the trigger.

The bolt flashed down the mountainside and buried itself in the rider's chest. He threw up his hands, grasping the air with rigid fingers, then slid off the horse's back and crashed to the ground.

The frightened horse plunged and reared. Puck watched through beady, crow eyes as it pranced along the path then, finding no master to halt it, galloped away, back down the mountain.

The sniper scrambled down the rocks, leaped onto the path, and approached the rider.

Taking a knife from his belt, he cut off one of the dead man's ears. This he placed in a small pouch attached to his belt. Then he dragged the body through a gap in the rocks beside the trail.

A deep crevasse yawned away below. With a grunt, he threw the body over the edge. It disappeared in silence.

The sniper stood. He looked up at the sky's reddened clouds. The light was fading.

He returned to the path. There he picked up his crossbow and began to climb up the rough mountain's slope. Past the ambush point he climbed, past the ledge above it, and up to a cave unseen from the trail.

Puck, balancing on the air currents, watched.

Soon a fire flared at the cave's entrance, and the smell of cooking venison was caught by the wind. It swirled a moment before it was dispersed among the peaks.

Puck found a suitable ledge and settled down for the night.

The next morning came cloudless and clear. The sun was rising into a gloriously blue sky when the sniper took up his position among the rocks. He had only a short time to wait.

Soon there came the sound of a traveller whistling, and of his staff striking the ground as he progressed.

The sniper raised the crossbow.

A strong, long-limbed adventurer walked jauntily into range. The sniper's finger tightened. The finger squeezed.

The bolt streaked faster than the eye could follow. It thudded into the adventurer's chest. He fell without a sound.

The sniper leaped down and ran to the corpse. He pulled out a knife. As he did so, he caught sight of the dead man's face. A gasp escaped him.

The dead man's face was his own!

How? The question played visibly over his face. But there was no doubting the eyes, the nose, the beard. Each was clearly his own.

Gritting his teeth, the sniper cut off an ear and put it into his pouch. Then he dragged the body through the gap in the rocks and pushed it over the edge. It vanished into the crevasse. Relief swept across his face as he watched it fall.

He turned, retrieved his bow, and again took up his place among the rocks.

The sky burnt. Sweat was squeezed from skin as the late morning heat shimmered off the rocks. So it was when another traveller came up the mountain pass.

This time it was a slight, middle-aged man. He wore peasant clothes, and a large floppy hat protected his face from the sun.

The sniper raised his bow.

The man tramped on.

The bolt flashed.

Without uttering a sound, the man fell.

Eagerly, the sniper scrambled down onto the trail. His knife glinted in his hand. Yet when he neared the dead man, he hesitated. Something ... something...

Nervous, he nudged the body with his foot, pushing the hat away from the face. And as he did so, he screamed. Once again the face was his own!

The sniper buried his face in his hands, looked up and down the trail, then, unable not to, glanced again at the dead man's face. It was his, without any doubt.

Trembling, he put away his knife without cutting off the ear. Groaning, he dragged the body through the gap in the rocks and let it fall into the crevasse. Shaking, he stared into the rocky depths long after it had vanished.

By degrees, he calmed himself. Finally, he stumbled back onto the path, picked up the crossbow, and returned to his seat in the rocks above the pass.

The day wore on. The sun rose to its zenith, burnt there for its allotted time, then started its slide into the afternoon. Heat wavered among the peaks. The sniper sat and waited.

Several hours later another traveller could be heard huffing and growling to himself. The sniper raised his bow. The traveller came on up the path, as yet hidden behind boulders. The sniper steadied his arm, waiting for the traveller to appear.

He came, swearing and cursing. He was a big man, as cragged as the mountains around him. His limbs were strong and tough, and a scruffy beard hung from his jaw.

The sniper watched him down the length of the bolt. The bolt followed as he strode on. The sniper's finger tightened on the trigger. But something about this traveller prevented him from shooting.

It was something familiar. The way he talked to himself, the way he walked, the ruggedness of his posture. An involuntary cry escaped the sniper's lips.

The traveller heard it. He halted. Deliberately, he revolved on his heel. His eyes sought out the source of the sound. His face lifted. His gaze met that of the sniper.

The sniper was looking at himself!

The sniper backed away, trying desperately to drag his eyes from the traveller's. But they followed him, ground into the depths of his heart. Shaking, the sniper scuttled up the mountainside. His frantic feet struck out for holds. His feverish fingers sought a desperate grip on the rocks.

From below, the traveller watched. The sniper vanished above. And the traveller waited.

Soon, a deathly scream echoed above. Followed by the sight of a falling body.

The sniper had shot himself with his crossbow. The bolt stuck out of the side of his neck. Blood spurted from the wound as the sniper's body bounced off rocks as it came crashing down the slope towards the pass.

The traveller watched as the sniper's body bounced on a large boulder above the path, then arced through a gap in the rocks and hurtled down into the crevasse.

The traveller drew his cloak about him, and twirled on his heel. The bearded traveller dissolved into the air, and the strong, long-limbed adventurer, the same as had come up the mountain that morning, took his place.

Puck looked a last time around the pass. Then he picked up his staff and continued on his way.

Nan-ku,
First of the Wise

One weakness too commonly bent the tongues of those who inhabited the Land of the Sad. This was the tendency to exaggerate. If something in that Land was good, it was called excellent, remarkable, wonderful. If bad, it was horrendous, terrible, the vilest tragedy since Ton-gu destroyed the Villages of Er and Orr.

Yet when Puck finally entered the village of Mik-un-Hunyar, to his surprise he discovered that this village was an exception to the general tendency. For it not only confirmed all that was said of it, but even surpassed it, such was its happy glow.

Situated in the middle of a fertile plain, on the banks of a glistening river, and surrounded by well-fruited trees and waving fields of grain, the village truly was affluent and peaceful.

In its sun-drenched square women sang as they wove cloth, ground corn, mended clothes, and watched their laughing children play. Out in the fields the men also sang as they unhurriedly worked, songs of faith, of hope, and of joy. But this world was not called the Land of the Sad without good reason. And if the village appeared to be a unique repository of laughter and light, yet beneath the rosiest skin a skeleton moves.

Thus, while Mik-un-Hunyar outwardly appeared to lack

the darker aspects which flowered so abundantly elsewhere, assuredly they were present here, too. It just took a little longer to find them. But find them Puck did.

Afternoon turned to dusk, and the village of Mik-un-Hunyar settled down to its evening meal. Soon the plates had been removed from the tables, the youngest children had been bedded, the evening mugs filled, and songs of thanks sung. Finally, an elderly man stood, signalled for silence, and spoke.

"People of Mik-un-Hunyar, we here are beloved of the Gods. In us rests satisfaction, peace, and happiness. This we all well know. And for it we daily give thanks."

The villagers banged their mugs on the tables in agreement.

"But why are we so blessed when others in this land lack even a fraction of what we possess? Brothers and sisters, it is because we each work hard to love the Gods and our fellow beings with all the power at our disposal. We send out our love, and that love is returned to us."

A murmur of agreement followed this statement.

"Of course," the elder continued, "this does not make us better than others. After all, everyone has a place in the plans of the Gods, even the wretched and the disposed. The Gods would not have given them existence were this not so. So be grateful, remain humble, and praise the Gods that our part should be so enchanted, and our daily life be so filled with delight."

And together the people of Mik-un-Hunyar knelt. And together they prayed. And, as one, their voices sent thanks to the great and compassionate Gods above.

They then washed their evening mugs, let the communal fire burn down, and made their yawning way to bed, content they had lived another day in accordance with the will of the Gods.

And Puck looked into their hearts as they drifted off to sleep. But what he saw there caused him to frown.

A crescent moon shone through the clouds. The wind sighed through the trees. In Mik-un-Hunyar, the sleeping villagers grunted and snored. All was restful, as befits those who lived in harmony with the good.

Yet, in the midst of this tranquillity, came the sound of a single twig snapping. Beneath the trees on the village outskirts stepped the shadowy form of a man. He looked around carefully, saw no-one, and slipped into one of the huts.

Inside, the intruder quietly looked through shelves, opened cupboards, and inspected drawers. Presently he came across a small bag lying in a corner of the kitchen, where it had apparently been tossed. The thief opened the bag and several gems spilled out onto his palm, gleaming in the moonlight. He grinned in satisfaction. However, just as he was about to slide the bag into his pocket, he was interrupted.

"Excuse me. I don't think I know you."

Candle-light transformed the intruder's grin into a flash of fear. He turned slowly to face the direction the voice had come from.

A woman stood in the doorway. Observing the thief's startled reaction, she smiled.

"I'm sorry. I didn't mean to alarm you. You're not from this valley, are you?"

The thief hesitated. He glanced at the doorway. He was closer to it than she was, which meant that if she tried anything, he had a clear line of escape.

Perceiving that this was his situation, the thief unstiffened a little. Turning back towards her, he slowly shook his head.

"I thought not," the woman observed. "That coat you're wearing is unlike any weaving I've seen. But please forgive me for being rude. My name is Nan-ku. Yours is ...?"

By now the thief had recovered himself sufficiently to

glance past the woman. He saw that the bedroom from which she had emerged held no one else. Nor was there stirring in any of the other rooms.

He spoke throatily. "I see you're here alone."

"My husband's on a hunting trip."

Nan-ku nodded at the thief's hand as he tried to slip the bag of gems unseen into his pocket. "You have our gems."

His hand tightened on it. "That's right. And if you shout to attract anyone's attention, I'll slit your throat from ear to ear."

And to back his threat, he drew a knife from his belt. But Nan-ku merely laughed.

"I wouldn't dream of shouting," she said. "I expect you're taking them because you need them more than we do."

The man cast a sideways glance at her, puzzled.

Nan-ku laughed. "No, I'm not crazy. It's just I noticed your clothes are old. And full of holes."

"That's right," he said. "My family don't have much. So I'm doing my bit to divvy up the odds."

Nan-ku thought about this.

"We're not wealthy. But we do have sufficient. Take the gems."

The thief grinned uneasily.

"I only ask you leave us the red one," she continued. "My husband found it in the mountains, and he plans to make a ring from it for his mother on her nameday."

The thief hesitated.

Nan-ku looked at him pleadingly. "Please?"

He shrugged. He opened the gem bag, stirred the gems inside with his fingers, and pulled out a red gem.

"Is this it?"

"It is. And I have something for you in exchange. It's cold around here at night."

She went to a cupboard, opened its door, and took out a coat, which she draped over a chair. "My husband hasn't worn it this year past."

She then went to another cupboard and took out a full wineskin, along with several pieces of dried meat, cheese, and bread. These she placed on the table, beside the coat. "For your journey."

Astonished, the thief stood rooted to the spot, only his head moving as he watched her cross the room to the bedroom door. There she paused, as if remembering something, and turned back to look at him.

"Close the front door after you, if you don't mind. Otherwise the goats come in and walk all over the furniture."

Then she re-entered the bedroom and closed the door.

The thief didn't need a second invitation. Gathering up all he had been offered, he paused only long enough to take a bag from behind the kitchen door, into which he stuffed his newly-acquired bounty. Then he was gone.

The next morning, Mik-un-Hunyar was abuzz with what had happened. Nan-ku's report on the incident had caused no upset. Rather, there was universal acclaim for the decision she had made.

"You've done Mik-un-Hunyar proud," the elder proclaimed when the villagers met for their noon meal. "What we have is not ours, but rather is given us by the Gods to caretake for our allotted time. By giving to those who ask, we do more than act as all responsible caretakers should."

That night, Mik-un-Hunyar slept in the knowledge that it was guided only by goodness and love.

All this Puck observed. Yet he knew that other attitudes than their own now rippled through the Land of the Sad. And these ripples would soon start lapping at the doors of a village which, until then, had lived so far from unease and storm. Then the incident occurred that changed all their lives forever.

The moon had set, and the night was at its darkest pass, when a prowler entered the village and darted into a hut. The prowler cast a cursory glance around the single central room, examining the shelves, and foraging roughly inside cupboards. His dissatisfied grunts indicated he could not find what he sought. He entered the bedroom and shook awake the woman who was sleeping in there.

"Give me your gems!" he commanded.

"What?" the shocked woman asked. "I don't have — "

The thief shoved a knife against her throat. "Don't lie to me!"

"Please I — "

Her cries clawed up to the heavens. But they found no purchase. They were the last sounds she made in this world.

Dawn found the stunned village gathered around the hut. Never before had such a tragedy occurred in the village of Mik-un-Hunyar. Never before had pain broken so forcefully into their village and shattered the tender fabric of their lives.

"How could this have happened?" was the repeated question. Their tear-filled eyes shifted from face to face. But they could do no more than sink to the ground and give voice to their grief.

Among them sat Nan-Ku. Too stupefied to cry, her heart ached with the greatest wound of all, it being her husband's mother to whom such a terrible deed had been done.

They were still seated, uncomprehending, around the hut when a villager approached holding aloft a ragged blood-stained coat.

"I found this beneath the trees over there," he cried. "It must have belonged to the murderer. Does anyone recognise it?"

All examined it and regretfully shook their heads. All, that is, but Nan-ku. Her reaction was of utter horror.

"I know who that belongs to," she said.

And she confessed that it was the same ragged coat as had been worn by the thief to whom she had given the gems and food.

Silence fell upon the village of Mik-un-Hunyar. The minutes passed as each villager considered the implications of Nan-ku's disclosure. Confusion, disbelief, incomprehension, doubt, and pain flittered alternatively across their faces.

For the truth was that never before had generosity cost those of Mik-un-Hunyar anything at all. While some of their livestock, and a few small items of food and possessions had previously been stolen, such losses were small matters, easily accommodated. Indeed, the fact they coped so easily merely bolstered the villagers' view of themselves as being naturally generous and beloved of the Gods. That was why Nan-ku's giving away of the gems had been so agreeable to them in the first instance. It confirmed that, as a village, they truly were good, generous, and true.

But this murder did not fit into these self-patting thoughts. For the death of a loved one was not a small matter, nor as easily accepted as a missing loaf of bread. Then the muttering began.

"If Nan-ku hadn't done what she did, we wouldn't be grieving here now."

"She should have foreseen," came the agreement.

"Generosity is all very well — "

" — but you're a fool if you don't count the cost to yourself."

"If she hadn't let that thieving murderer go — "

"Enough!"

The village elder stood. All eyes turned towards him.

"We villagers of Mik-un-Hunyar are better than this!"

The hubbub of voices fell away. But pursed mouths and fierce eyes revealed the intensity of feeling that remained. The elder poured his words onto the villagers' seething rage.

"We were not with Nan-ku when she gave what she did to the intruder. But we all agreed that she had done what was loving and right. We even applauded her actions in this very place. So how is it just for us to condemn her now?"

A few villagers complained at this question. But more looked down and nodded their heads.

"Love is not a gift to be shared only in easy times. If it was enough for us to support Nan-ku previously, it is enough to support her now."

Nodding became general. And even the doubters offered no contrary words. Yet the day's events were not yet over. For at this moment in the discussion, another villager approached.

"I have more terrible news. Brace yourself, Nan-ku." He turned to face the her. "Your husband is also dead."

And with a cry, Nan-ku collapsed.

It was only much later that she was capable of hearing and absorbing what had happened. Her husband's body had been discovered in a ditch edging the village's fields. And not only had Nan-ku's husband died the same night as his mother, he had also been stabbed in exactly the same place. The conclusion was unavoidable. The same man had murdered them both. And this man was the intruder to whom Nan-ku had given so much!

Not a word was spoken as the villagers digested this news. All understood the pain this revelation was causing Nan-ku. They also grappled with the implications of their shared generosity, that had led to the deaths of two of their own.

But for Nan-ku the implications were a knife that buried itself deeper and deeper inside her with each passing minute.

And she knew what she had to do.

That night, Nan-ku gathered clothing and food. And, without another word, she walked away from the village of Mik-un-Hunyar. Those she had been born among, with whom she had grown up, who had celebrated the wedding of her and her husband, who had enjoyed her joy and laughter, never saw her kind eyes again.

Yet she was not unseen. For Puck had witnessed all that had happened. And he watched over Nan-ku as she walked through the night and when, for the first time in her life, she lay down to sleep under the open sky, washed by the cold light of the stars. He shared her feeling of utter aloneness as she wept. And he listened as, after her weeping had run its course, she uttered a lament.

"You Gods above, I acted out of good, and evil resulted. Is this the reality of the world you have created for us?"

With tear-filled eyes she stared up at the heavens.

"You see and know everything. So answer this one question: Do my actions have any goodness in them? Or is all filled with purposelessness and evil?"

She kept looking up. And waited. The wind blew. The leaves rustled. The cold starlight rippled. But no response reached down to touch her from the realm of the Gods.

Nan-ku lowered her head. She wrapped the cloak tighter around her shoulders, closed her unsleeping eyes, and lay there, feeling no answer. Yet she had been heard. Not by the Gods, but by Puck, their emissary. And he did what he had been commanded to do.

Time passed. Each day Nan-ku journeyed further from the village of Mik-un-Hunyar. And she saw many things for the first time. Things she had never previously imagined could even exist in the land beyond her own.

She passed villages where babies cried all day.

She passed houses where young children went hungry, and squares where girls stared narrow-eyed at other girls.

She observed hillsides where boys goaded one another without thought, and ponds where bent women washed clothes, then struggled to straighten their backs at the day's exhausted end.

She walked through fields where men glared at her knowingly, yet knew nothing of how life was in the next village.

And she sat in graveyards where only the dead did not complain about the time life demanded they spend there.

And soon sadness set up house in her heart. Not sadness for herself, but sadness for all those others who had never known a soft touch. Had never felt the spreading peace of dusk. Had never smelt the kind perfume of a smile. Had never been where they were wholly wanted and loved. And in this she understood the extent to which, without being aware of it, she had been privileged all the years of her dwelling in the village of Mik-un-Hunyar.

Then an event occurred that puzzled her all over again. She had been walking across low hills, where the grass was bitten down, and a handful of skinny sheep wandered desultorily. Nan-ku then noticed a small village, and its busy market, among a knoll of trees below. She hesitated. Her destination today was a large village visible in the distance, beside the shimmering waters of a lake. She had no intention of halting. Yet a thought flitted through her mind that she should descend to the village.

She considered the idea. Her mouth was dry, and her water flask was only half full. And as it was still only midday, she had plenty of time to reach her destination before nightfall. The idea came to her that a brief rest would do her good. So she turned from the path.

A song immediately started singing itself inside her as she walked, a song that made its leaping way into her heart. But what she did not feel was the hand of the invisible Puck, hovering behind her, gently nudging her down the slope towards the market.

Shirts, trousers, skirts, jackets, shoes, bed coverings, pottery, and rugs hung in lines of stalls. The smell of sweet toffee and fried breads hung in the air. Nan-ku spotted a brewer of teas and started walked towards him. Abruptly, she froze.

Reason told her it couldn't possibly be so. But she found herself staring at a coat that was exactly like the one her husband had owned, the coat she had given to the intruder that fatal night. It was draped over the shoulders of a young woman who had paused before a stall containing children's clothing.

Curious, Nan-ku walked towards the woman. And her surprise compounded further because she was now caught up in a familiar lanolin smell. Her husband had regularly rubbed all his coats with sheep's fat to help keep them waterproof. Of course, this was a common practice and no proof that the coat was her husband's.

However, her husband had once fallen into a river while hunting, and rocks had ripped the coat's arm. Nun-ku had mended the tear, but it had created a distinctive line of herring bone stitches down the coat's left arm. So her husband's coat possessed a unique blemish.

To assure herself that this definitely was not her husband's coat, Nan-ku stepped around the woman to view the left arm. She instantly saw the familiar herring bone stitching. It was her husband's!

The woman glanced up. "Is something wrong?"

Nan-ku was flustered. "Yes. No. I was just – your coat."

"A gift from my brother," the woman explained. "Don't ask

me where he got it. He traded it somewhere. It's not elegant. But I get chilly. In my condition, you see."

The woman turned. And Nan-ku did see. The woman's bulging front revealed she was in the last weeks of pregnancy.

"This is my third," the woman explained. "The first two were easy, but this one is drinking all my warmth."

"I know how unlikely this sounds," Nan-ku responded. "But my husband once owned that very coat. I'm curious to know how your brother came by it. Could you possibly ask him about it?"

"My brother's name is Tu-raq. You should ask him yourself."

That was how Nan-ku met Me-war. And that was how Nan-ku came to be seated at the table in Me-mar's kitchen, drinking hot spiced apple juice, when the door opened and Tu-raq walked in.

The moment he saw Nan-ku, he stopped short. He remained rooted to the spot, not saying a word, as Me-war introduced him. He was still staring silently at Nan-ku some time after Me-war had finished.

"Tu-raq, don't be rude. Say hello to our guest."

Finally, Tu-raq emerged from his reverie.

"Have we ever met before?" he asked Nan-ku.

"No," she replied.

"Yet last night I saw you. In a dream. You were seated in that exact chair."

Me-war explained. "We are a family of dreamers. But we normally dream of other people, and of other places."

"Until last night I had never dreamed of this house," Tu-raq confirmed.

Me-war nodded. "Your dream must be a sign from the Gods."

A moment after she uttered these words, an ornament that had been on the sideboard shattered on the tile floor. Their three heads turned to see the broken pieces on the floor, and the curtains beside the headboard flapping.

"I'll close the window," Tu-raq observed.

He stepped forwards, then halted, puzzled. The window was already shut.

Standing invisibly beside the sideboard, Puck withdrew his hand from the curtain and chuckled to himself.

"Don't worry," Me-war said nonchalantly to Nan-ku. "This house isn't haunted."

"Except by the past," Tu-raq added.

"The past?" Nan-ku asked.

"Me-war's husband disappeared three moons ago. We know he is dead. We've grieved. Now it is over."

"That's another coincidence," Nan-ku observed. "My husband also died a little more than three moons ago."

"It's strange how today rushes into the past, and is gone forever," Me-war observed. "Yet we carry the past with us always."

"It's the past I wish to discuss with you," said Nan-ku. "I feel I have to tell you my story."

Brother and sister sat. And Nan-ku described how Me-war's coat had been her husband's. How she had given it away one might to an intruder who had broken into their house. And how the same man had returned and broken into another home, which belonged to her husband's mother, who he had killed. And how the body of her husband was found in the fields the next morning, presumably a victim of the same intruder. This was the man who left behind a tattered jerkin, and had worn her husband's coat. Which Me-war had been wearing in the market that day.

Me-war and Tu-raq turned to look at the coat.

"What I want to know," Nan-ku concluded, "is who was the intruder I took pity on and helped, and who repaid my act of kindness with one of evil. I need to find him so I can ask him why he it is he could do such a thing."

"I think we should rid ourselves of the coat," Me-war said. "It's tainted with blood. It will taint this house and us."

"I'd gladly help you burn it right now," Nan-ku replied.

"No," said Tu-raq. "That's not the right use for it."

"You wish to wear it yourself, brother?"

"Think on what has happened here. Of all the places in the Land of the Sad that coat and Nan-ku could have gone to, they have both ended up in this house, at the same time. It is as if Nan-ku's feet had been led here. I think — "

Abruptly, Tu-raq launched himself full-length across the room, hand out-stretched. He caught a second ornament a moment before it hit the floor.

"Alright," he said as he stood, placing the ornament back on the sideboard, and looking around the room, "I don't know who you are. But we get the point."

And the curtains fluttered in acknowledgement.

Nan-ku stared astounded at the curtains as they gradually stilled themselves. But Me-war just shrugged.

"Such things happen from time to time."

"If I may finish making my point," Tu-raq said. "Of all the places Nan-ku and her husband's coat might have gone to, both arrived here, in this house of dreamers."

Nan-ku was further intrigued. "What do you mean, house of dreamers?"

"I mean," Tu-raq replied, "that I can dream the coat's journey. Following the coat's scent trail, I can journey in dream into the past and discover all that happened to the coat that brought it here."

Suddenly Nan-ku understood the point Tu-raq had been making. "You can do that?"

"I can."

"So," Nan-ku said, half to herself, "I have been brought here that my cry to the Gods might be answered."

Me-war and Tu-raq exchanged a knowing look.

"When do we start?" Nan-ku asked eagerly.

"Tonight."

The day passed. Dusk arrived. And with it came the promise of Tu-raq's dreamed journey of discovery.

Yet when the sun had set, and the evening meal had been eaten, and the lamp's wick had been lowered, and all had lain down to sleep, it was not Tu-raq who dreamed the coat's journey. It was Nan-ku, transported by the power of Puck.

Nun-ku woke in her dream to find herself back in the village of Mik-un-Hunyar. But this time she was hovering above it, looking down as the intruder backed out of her hut. She watched as he quickly ran out of the village, and into the trees that stood between the huts and the fields.

The scene shifted. Now she was floating high among branches, looking down, watching as the intruder ran through the woods. He jumped a narrow stream, raced around a bend in the path, and ran straight into two men.

Their response was immediate. They knocked him down, stripped him of his clothing, and bound him with twine.

Next they went through his belongings, where they found the bag of gems. A fight immediately broke out between the two robbers, a vicious whirl of fists, grunts, and blood. It left one unconscious in the dirt, and the other triumphantly holding the bag of gems as he scampered into the undergrowth.

Nan-ku was abruptly much closer to the ground, watching as the remaining robber recovered consciousness. He sat up groggily as he regained his bearings. Then he saw the bound and naked intruder.

He pulled the gag from the intruder's mouth and demanded to be told the name of the village from which he had obtained the gems. Initially, the intruder refused to speak. But two well-placed punches, and the now broken-nosed intruder told all. The robber then ran off, across the stream, and into the wood.

Time passed. The sun was setting as yet another man came walking through the wood. He walked with a familiar gait. In the dream, Nan-ku started. It was Nan-ku's husband!

But even before she could respond to this realisation, he had discovered his own coat lying beside the path. He quickly spotted the bound intruder. He untied his bonds, and they spoke briefly. Then Nan-ku's husband picked up his own coat, jumped the stream, and disappeared in the same direction the robber had followed.

Yet again the scene changed. Red dawn light was beginning to touch the sky. And Nan-ku was back in the fields outside the village of Mik-un-Hunyar. And this time her husband was lying on the ground, completely still, and the thief was pulling a knife from deep in his throat.

As Nan-ku watched, she saw a ghostly smudge detach itself from her husband's body, linger a few moments above its immobile physical form, then lift away and disappear into the sky.

The thief picked up the coat and ran off into the night.

A rush of images followed, of the coat changing hands. It ended in the market that afternoon, when Nan-ku had seen Me-war with the coat draped over her shoulders.

But the dream had not yet finished. Because she was suddenly hovering on a mountain pass, looking down at the thatched roof of a large house. The courtyard outside the house was full of children. Nan-ku had the feeling these children were all orphans. She dropped closer, and saw the slightly stooped back of a man who was playing with the children. She didn't know the significance of this house, or who the man was. But she knew she had to go there.

Nan-ku woke. She was immediately assailed by a complex of thoughts and emotions. If her dream of the coat's journey had any veracity, the man she thought was responsible for the deaths of her husband and his mother was not. In addition, if her husband's path through the woods had not crossed that of the bound intruder, he would most likely still be alive. And the coat's presence in the home of Tu-raq and Me-war appeared to be an accident of trade.

Yet she remained the cause of what had happened. If she had not generously allowed the intruder to leave with the gems, the robbers would not have found them, fought, and one would not have come to Mik-un-hunyar in search of gems for himself. So no deaths would have resulted.

On the other hand, Nan-ku knew that she had been generous from childhood. It was her nature to be so. So if she was the cause, the only way of not setting in train the events that occurred would have been for her not to be herself.

Nan-ku lay in the darkness, listening to Me-war's family softly breathing, thinking on all this. As she did, Puck flew overhead. And Nan-Ku had a vision.

Nan-Ku's vision was of a vast web of strands, some black, some white, with many coloured between. All these strands were interwoven, together creating a huge entwined lace of actions that stretched from the past and disappeared into the future. Nan-ku saw herself surrounded by this vast sea of undulating intertwined strands, with numbers of coloured strands passing through her, forwards and behind, as she walked towards her own future. And she could do no more than wonder.

At times apparently inexplicable events occurred in the Land of the Sad. Some rose naturally out of the nature of life in that world, while others had no immediately discernible cause.

One of these events took place in Me-war's house the next morning.

As the family prepared breakfast, a villager appeared at the door. He had news. Me-war's husband body had been found in a ravine at the foot of distant mountains. He had been killed by the bolt from a crossbow, and most of his body had subsequently been eaten by animals and birds. The state of the body meant that it had to be buried where it was found.

Me-war made no sound in response to this news. Instead, she marched into the hallway, took Nan-ku's husband's coat off its hook, walked outside with it, threw it on the ground, placed kindling on top of it, and set it on fire.

Only when it was nothing but ash did she return inside to hear what else the messenger had to say. Me-war's husband had been travelling as a courier, and all the goods he was carrying with him at the time of his death were still with his body. Attempts had been made to trace the man whose good's Me-war's husband was transporting, but he had disappeared. So those goods now belonged to Me-war.

The messenger gave her two bags, and left. Me-war and Nan-ku watched as Tu-raq opened them. In one were a specially embroidered wedding dress, hand painted scarfs, and two ornately hand-carved flutes, all labelled with a village and recipient.

The second bag contained bread and cheese, which had gone stale. But under the food, at the very bottom, was a small package. This small bag held the greatest surprise. It was the same bag of gems Nan-ku had given the intruder!

Nan-ku stared in shock at the gems lying on the table. The

early morning sun hit them, sending out a prism of colours –
red, green, purple, yellow – that lit up the corner of the table,
a portion of wall, and Nan-ku's own face. She stared blankly at
them, barely comprehending what she was seeing.

But at that moment the curtains behind her shivered. And
an idea crystalised in Nan-ku's mind. She stood.

"These are my husband's gems," she said. "And I know exactly where they must go."

Nan-ku swept all the gems into their carry bag, gathered
her possessions, and hugged Me-war and Tu-raq farewell. After
promising to return as soon as she was able, Nan-ku walked up
the path to the ridge above the village.

There she paused, at the same point she had halted the previous day, wondering which way she should go. She remained
there for some time, waiting for a sign.

Clouds scudded across the sky above. Birds fluttered past.
Sheep browsed on the short grass, while others sat in the shade
of a clump of trees, chewing.

Then a curious event occurred. There was no wind. Yet a
number of dead leaves near Nan-ku's feet suddenly lifted into
the air and were carried back in the direction from which she
had come the day before. Nan-ku turned in that direction, and
started walking.

Three days later Nan-ku was standing on a ridge, looking
down at the same thatched roof she had seen in her dream. She
descended and walked through the gates and into a courtyard
full of children. And there, standing among them, was the man
in her dream. As then, his back was turned towards her.

He must have become aware of her presence, because he
put down the child he was holding and swung around. As Nan-
ku had been expecting, she recognised his face. The man was
the intruder to whom she had originally given the gems.

He recognised her immediately. A flash of fear passed across his face. Then he saw her face conveyed neither anger nor rancour, and his expression softened. He walked over to her.

"I am sorry for all that happened to you and your family," he said. "It was my fault. If I hadn't entered your house — "

"None of us can know where the ifs in our life will lead."

"As you can see, in shame I gave up that life. I am now the carer of these orphans."

"So if you had not done what you did then, you would not be where you are now?"

"No. But I still ask you your forgiveness — "

"Then no more needs to be said. I have something that belongs to you."

Nan-ku held out her hand. It was the bag of gems.

"I gave them to you once. And I can never take them back." Nan-ku nodded towards the children. "Besides, it appears you have the greater need."

Tears stood in the man's eyes.

"I know what you're thinking," Nan-ku said feelingly. "So there is no need to speak."

They stood in silence as the children played in the yard.

"Can I persuade you to stay tonight?" the man asked. But he already knew the answer.

"I had a dream last night," Nan-ku said, "of a house I am called to find."

And she turned and walked out of the courtyard and into the hills that surrounded the orphanage.

Five days later, as warm dusk light filtered through leaves, Nan-ku stood on one side of a clearing, looking at a house standing beside a cooling stream. Inside the house, a woman could be heard wailing.

Nan-ku crossed the clearing and approached the house.

But what she wasn't aware of was Puck was hovering over her. And as she halted at the door to knock, Puck dropped an invisible cloak across her shoulders. This cloak came from the Starways, and was woven from the sighs of the Gods. It was given out rarely, and only to those who walked through the valley of suffering, and discovered what resided on its far side.

Nan-ku opened the door, and walked in. The door closed gently behind her. Presently, the woman's wailing stopped.

And so Puck left Nan-ku to live out the rest of her days. And in time she came to be known as Nan-ku, First of the Wise.

Pale Humans,
Dark Gods

*P*uck decided he should explore the Mountains of What Cannot Be. And so it was that he discovered The Valley of the Never Was. It proved to be a sombre place, its sky covered by heavy clouds that threatened a storm. Intrigued, Puck paused to investigate the lives of those who chose to live there.

The village he entered was bleak. The sun had been pushed behind thick cloud, leaving the day chilled by a blustery wind that ferreted at his clothing. The village streets gave the impression of being exhausted, with the house walls grey and beaten, and the air heavy with lassitude and despair.

Outside one house, Puck noticed a raggedly dressed child sitting in the mud. Even as Puck observed, a dishevelled woman came out of the house, picked up the child and, after glancing suspiciously at Puck, carried him inside. The door banged after her.

Puck turned to look at the street in which he stood. Mud walls crowded together along both sides of the street. Elsewhere in the Land of the Sad, wooden doors opened to invite entrance. But all these doors were firmly closed against any visitors.

As Puck walked down the street, he saw on either side dismal walls, curtained windows, and hunched roofs. A thin, mange-eaten dog skulked down an alley, its red eyes gazing hungrily at Puck, worn tail between its legs.

Yet, despite the appearance of abandonment, people did live here. Puck caught sight of a child gazing from a curtained window. Then he noticed an elderly, bent woman hurrying out of a doorway and across the road. She disappeared through a second doorway, and again the door snapped shut behind her.

Puck looked up. On either side of the village rose steep mountain slopes. They gave the impression the village was held in the palm of some great malevolent force that only had to draw the fingers of its peaks together to engulf it utterly.

Soon Puck reached the edge of a large square. There, on its far side, facing the snow-capped peaks, was an altar. To Puck's surprise, a child lay on the altar. And an ornate dagger hovered over the child's breast. The child squirmed. But ropes attached to the little girl's wrists and ankles held her fast.

"Halt!" Puck shouted.

Three figures dressed in black robes stood behind the altar. At the shout they looked up. But one who wore a red hat signalled for the ceremony to continue. The dagger plunged.

There was only a split second in which to act. So Puck performed the one action he had time to carry out. He cast a spell.

The dagger froze in its downward stroke. It trembled just a finger's width from the poor child's chest.

No one moved as Puck approached.

The waist-high altar was embossed with squiggled lettering and swirling forms. Those arrayed around it, frozen where they stood, regarded Puck with mixed expressions of rage and fear as he walked slowly towards them. Yet their powers of speech had not been restricted. The head priest, distinguished by a high red hat, made use of this state immediately.

"I command you to undo what you have done!" he shouted.

"The sacrifice must be completed. Release us this instant, or you shall be sacrificed as well!"

Puck looked from one wide-eyed face to the other.

The girl lay shivering in the middle of the altar. Puck reached down and untied the ropes which bound her. As she immediately sprang up.

"It's alright," Puck told her gently. "You can go home now."

"You mustn't do this!" the head priest directed. "They'll destroy us all!"

But Puck's spell prevented any from moving. Helping the girl off the altar, Puck wrapped his own cloak around her chilled body.

"Go home," he said gently.

Without pausing to glance at the priests, the girl scampered across the square. Puck watched as a door opened, and she ran inside.

Puck then turned his eyes up towards the mountain peaks that towered over them all.

As if aware of his gaze, a flash of lightning lit the dark clouds around the peaks. This was followed by a clap of thunder. The wind blowing off the peaks intensified for a moment, spinning a cruel chilly blast around those gathered below. The day, like this village, was dying.

Puck turned back to the priests.

"Will you explain yourself?" the head priest demanded.

Puck eyed the priest distastefully.

"We priests of the Valley of the Never Was," the priest continued, "are not known for our patience."

"I'd have thought," Puck replied, "that a sorcerer from the far side of the Brooding Dark would warrant more respect than this."

A gasp went up from the priests. Clearly, while they lived

far from other villages, they had heard of such sorcerers, who were rumoured to be the most powerful in the Land of the Sad. When the head priest spoke again, there was a new respect in his voice.

"We beg your pardon, powerful one. But you must realise the difficult predicament we are in."

Puck raised his eyebrows. "I do not. Tell me. Why were you sacrificing the child?"

"Because the Dark Gods demand it."

"And who are the Dark Gods?"

"The Valley of the Never Was exists in the shadows of the Mountains of What Cannot Be. Among their peaks live the Dark Gods. Periodically, the Dark Gods send down avalanches and storms which decimate our crops and kill our people."

"So you offer sacrifices to the Dark Gods to appease them in the hope that they will not destroy your future crops?"

Tears filled the head priest's eyes. "We don't like to do it. But there is no other way."

"Where do the Dark Gods come from?"

"Nobody knows," replied the priest.

"And has anyone seen these Dark Gods?"

"Of course we don't see them. They are Gods. But every day we see their effects."

Puck waved his hand and broke the spell.

The priests slumped to the ground. The head priest straightened the red hat on his head, and looked pleadingly at Puck.

"You have to help us. Without the sacrifice, the Dark Gods will surely come down and destroy us."

And the heavy skies around the mountain peaks flashed and thundered, as if in agreement.

During this conversation a few doors had opened hesitantly, and villagers began trickling out. Now they drifted across the square like opaque spectres. Soon one hundred men, women and children stood in a mute semi-circle a short distance from the altar.

Puck noted their stooped bodies, their lank hair, their pinched faces, their pale, defeated eyes. And his heart filled.

"Do you want to escape these Dark Gods?"

A hubbub of voices leapt in reply.

"We dare not even think on it," the head priest responded. "They are too powerful."

And the gathered crowd murmured their assent.

"Perhaps the Dark Gods have their powers," said Puck. "But we magicians from the far side of the Brooding Dark are not without power of our own. I assure you that my spells can rid you of the Dark Gods forever."

The villagers shifted uneasily, muttering as they deliberated on Puck's words. The head priest recovered his balance first. But now, as he spoke, his voice was filled with both awe and doubt.

"But the Dark Gods have more than mortal power."

"So do I," Puck replied.

And without waiting for further comment, Puck stepped towards the Mountains of What Cannot Be. The villagers shuffled away, bunching in a tight group behind the priest.

Before Puck rose the indomitable mountain walls. He raised his arms towards the skies and mouthed softly to himself the secret name of the Gods.

For a short time nothing happened.

Then, without warning, the skies were split by a cacophonous explosion. The clouds were torn apart, and a hole appeared. For the first time in many years the setting Sun was seen hanging over the snow-capped Mountains of What Cannot Be.

Puck turned back to face the villagers. Now he was surprised. Because they were all kneeling on the ground, their foreheads in the dirt. Even the head priest kept his eyes averted as he spoke.

"Forgive our doubts. We had no way of knowing how powerful you are."

"Take your faces out of the dirt," Puck replied kindly. "I'm no god to be worshipped."

Obediently, the villagers stood.

"Now, tell me," Puck addressed them. "Do you, or do you not, wish me to rid you of your Dark Gods?"

The villagers instantly gathered into a knot and discussed the offer. Voices argued, shouted, agreed and disagreed. Presently, silence fell. The head priest turned to Puck.

"We are agreed. We wish to be rid of the Dark Gods forever."

With a solemn motion, Puck waved his arm. A spell was cast. In the square the villagers waited.

Behind them stretched their shadows, thrown out by the setting Sun. Yet even as they watched and waited, something strange started to happen. For although the villagers were all still, their shadows began to move.

Abruptly, screams shattered the air as the shadows detached themselves from the villagers' feet and begun attacking their owners' bodies!

People scattered across the square, some with shadows seated on their chests, choking their throats, others fighting off their shadows with kicks, punches, and bites. Several ran into houses, pursued by implacable dark shapes. Other villagers lay on the ground, silent and still.

"What have you done!" the head priest cried.

But the situation was already changing.

For during the intervening minutes the Sun had continued to slide across the sky. And now its orb was rapidly sinking behind the towering snow-covered peaks. And as the Sun did so, the villagers' shadows began to lose their intensity. In another minute they started softening.

Soon, the Sun disappeared completely behind the peaks, and the marauding shadows dissolved.

Terror left the villagers' bodies. Relief expressed itself in hugs and weeping.

While, high above, the clouds continued to clear. In a few minutes the sky became perfectly clear. For the first time in generations, the villagers saw the crescent moon rise above the horizon, and the first flickerings of the night sky's stars.

Puck waited for the villagers to absorb all that had just happened. Then, when he had their attention, he spoke again.

"I promised to rid you of the Dark Gods. As you have discovered, the Dark Gods do not exist up there, in the mountain peaks. Rather, they exist here below, among you all. Be assured your shadows will never again rise up against you all as they did today. But you cannot relax. For, in future, your shadows will be far more cunning and subtle. In future you will find them in your speech, in your thoughts, in your acts."

Puck looked at the villagers, giving them a moment to absorb his words. Then he continued.

"Whether your future existence will be better or worse than the lives you have had until now, I leave you each to decide. But know that even in the blackest night, where neither sun, nor moon, nor torchlight reaches, your shadows shall never leave your sides. I leave your priests to discover and explain all this in greater detail."

Filled with wonder and relief, some among the villagers began dismantling the altar on which so many deaths had occurred. Others gathered together their families, and made their shaky way back to their homes.

The priests remained in a huddle as they consulted briefly. The head priest then approached Puck. He deeply bowed.

"We thank you, sorcerer," the priest said. "Your help here cannot be repaid. But is there anything at all we can do for you?"

"The return of my cloak is sufficient."

Puck accepted from the young girl's grateful and teary-eyed mother the cloak he had earlier placed around her daughter's shoulders.

Then he turned and walked away, into the Mountains of What Cannot Be, where he was soon swallowed by the crouching darkness.

The Dream Thief

Puck was seated one evening in an ale-house, wearing the body of a seller of herbs and medicines. A satchel full of those products lay on the floor beside him, while around him were people from all walks of life in the Land of the Sad. Farmers, carpenters, crafts people, teachers, store-keepers, travelling couriers, bakers, clothing makers, and merchants sat shoulder to shoulder, consuming ale amid vivacious chatter.

Puck was enjoying this atmosphere when a young man with elaborately curled moustaches sat down at the table beside him. The young man nodded to Puck. Puck nodded back. And a conversation was struck up.

The young man introduced himself as Si-mung, a donkey-trainer. Puck replied that he was a dealer in medicinal herbs. Common ground was soon found. Both had an interest in travel. So each recounted a favourite travelling adventure. Then, the conversation took an unexpected turn.

Leaning confidently towards Puck, Si-Mung lowered his voice and offered a confession.

"Someone has been stealing my dreams."

This was one of the most interesting statements Puck had heard uttered by the sons and daughters of the Earth.

"Tell me more," he immediately requested.

Si-mung explained. His family had long possessed a special faculty for dreaming. Not every member of the family, just one or two in each generation. And Si-mung was the one from among his cousins. What this faculty gave was an ability to dream of far away places, of strange and mysterious worlds, wherein beings other than humans lived, evolved and died. But the dreamer not only saw these places, he became an active part of them. All that happened in those worlds was therefore as vivid and as real as what happened to him in the Land of the Sad.

Si-mung went on to describe how, in his dream travels, wisdom was given to him, usually wisdom of that world, but sometimes wisdom regarding the workings of his own. So it had been for others in his family, and so for several years it had continued for him. Then, one day, all this began to change.

He remembered clearly the dream during which the change first became apparent. He was in a strange and extraordinary world, in which the dominant beings occupied four-armed, no-legged bodies, and lived in trees. They were small creatures, with furry faces and shrill voices. Si-mung said he was wearing one of their bodies, swinging through the tree-tops with them, across a valley filled with red-leafed trees and gigantic, orange-smelling flowers, when the change began.

It was subtle at first, being merely a lack of focus on the extreme edges of his vision. But then forms on the horizon vanished, as if they were being sucked away. The vanishing spread rapidly across the dreamscape.

Soon it was the world nearer to him which was sucked away, then the valley directly beneath. The other beings around him were next, and finally he felt his own body being sucked off him. In a moment he was a disembodied awareness floating in the void, where there were no forms, no sensations, no feelings, nothing whatsoever. Then he felt himself falling back into his earthly body. He hit it, and woke.

So it had continued since that date. Gradually, more and more of his dreams were stolen while he was in the middle of them. Until now every dream was. Here Si-mung's confession ended.

Puck considered briefly. He then leaned towards Si-mung.

"I can help you," he said.

"You can?" Si-mung asked excitedly.

"Through my herbs."

And Puck described a special mixture of herbs, the effects of which were such that when two people drank of them, one could enter into the dreams of the other. Puck suggested that they should drink of those herbs, and that he would then enter Si-mung's dreams and observe what happened.

"That's exactly what I need!" Si-mung exclaimed.

It was decided they would meet again, one week hence, at that very same inn. During that period Puck would collect and prepare the necessary concoction. The two shook hands and went their separate ways.

The following week saw them arrived back at the inn. They hired a room for the night, then whiled away the time with conversation until it was the hour to retire. That hour struck and they entered the room, eager for adventure.

Each in turn drank of Puck's herb mixture. Naturally, it was merely a harmless relaxant. Because of his power, Puck did not need to resort to herbal intervention to fulfil his plan. But he did not want to frighten Si-mung, and so maintained this facade.

They lay down to sleep. Si-mung was soon breathing in a slow, even rhythm.

Puck rose out of his body and entered Si-mung's dream. Instantly, he found himself in a remarkable world.

His first impression was of a bird singing. Its song was soft and lilting, sobbing almost. It sang the history of its kind, how they came down from the skies and entered the bodies of a race of birds. How they later became trapped in those bodies and were unable to escape. How, finally, despairing and heart-broken, they chose to kill themselves and leave only a few songsters behind to tell of their plight and end. The notes hung mournfully on the air, dispersing in a final sigh.

Meanwhile, by degrees, sight came to Puck. With far greater intensity and focus than in an ordinary dream, forms coagulated out of the void, shapes solidified. The world around him took on the sharpness of reality, of which he too became a living part. Puck looked on with admiration, greatly enjoying all that he perceived.

There was no vegetation or animal life in this world. All was crystalline. And all was five-fold in construction. Every form had five points to it, or five faces, or was grouped into five, which, in turn, was part of another large grouping of five.

Flower-like growths started up from rocky masses, all structured on the basis of five. Similarly there were fern-like arrangements, and other forms which looked somewhat like trees. Yet all were solidified into a crystalline existence.

Colours shone there, again five in number: red, yellow, green, blue, and a deep violet. The colours shifted continuously through the crystals, creating an eerie sense of imbalance. While, high above, the deep blue sky was dominated by a huge, red sun which hung just above the horizon, but cast neither shadow and nor heat.

His inspection over, Puck flew into the sky and began to search both for Si-mung and the source of the song.

He found them together.

Far below was a small mountain, on one side of which sat

the bird. It was transparent. Through it Puck could see the co-lours shifting within the mountain. The bird too was crystal-line, yet in the middle of its breast a tiny white light pulsed. The song drifted out of its mouth and hung mournfully on the air.

And hovering beside it, a ghostly semi-transparent pres-ence, was Si-mung.

The bird sang to Si-mung, the same sad story Puck had already heard and interpreted. But Si-mung was slower than Puck, so the bird was repeating it, more carefully, and more simply. Puck watched them for an instant, then flew off. For, he had become aware of another presence in this world.

He departed in the direction of his impression, across the petrified landscape which stretched lifelessly beneath him, over the dead flowers and trees, past cold symmetries which spoke of an existence long annexed from the alive, in which all was now static and fixed. Which made this other presence, in that it was alive and moving, definitely alien to this realm.

Puck hovered. Guessing at the presence's location, he de-scended. And presently he caught sight of what he sought.

The being was hovering above a cluster of green and violet crystals which had once been, in that world's maturity, a clump of trees. He was a small blemish among the bright colours, a shadowy form from another world.

Puck approached him. The being bowed in acknowledg-ment of his arrival.

"Greetings," said the being.

"Greetings," Puck replied.

The being held a bag in his hands. Puck indicated it.

"Is that where you place Si-mung's stolen dreams?"

The being nodded.

"Why do you do so?" Puck asked.

"Because it is the task the Gods have given me."

Puck paused. He considered.

"Truly," said Puck, after he had considered, "if you are a servant of the Gods, it is not for me to interfere with anything you do."

The being nodded. "You are wise, Puck of the Starways."

"How is it you know who I am?"

"A speaker for the Gods said we would meet one day. I am Ra-Herm, dream collector."

"I'm pleased to meet you, Ra-Herm. Yet I am not sufficiently wise to understand the purpose of the Gods in commanding you to steal Si-mung's dreams. Can you tell me why that is?"

"Certainly," said Ra-Herm. "When the Gods transformed the Land of the Happy into the Land of the Sad, they also gave humanity dreams. In particular, they gave humanity the ability to dream not merely of what is for them in their lives, but of what is not yet, but that one day might be. Yet while all in the Land of the Sad dream, few manage to make their dreams real. My task is to collect all those dreams which remain unused, and which would otherwise be wasted. That is my task as dream collector, first class."

"You do well," said Puck. "But what then of Si-mung? Why do you steal his dreams when they are far from those which humankind ordinarily dreams?"

"Si-mung is certainly gifted," the Ra-Herm replied. "I have never, in all my travels, witnessed such dreams. But," and here he lowered his voice, as if fearful of being overheard, "some being who serves the Gods has witnessed Si-mung's dreams. And I have been ordered to pay special attention to him."

"Why so?"

"Because Si-mung is satisfied with small dreams. He has not yet dreamed of being among the Gods. I have been ordered to steal those small dreams that he may eventually dream the big dream. When he does so, he will be beyond my power and will have achieved what the Inconceivable decreed."

Puck bowed to Ra-Herm.

"I thank you for your wisdom."

Ra-Herm bowed in return. He then opened the shadowy bag in his hand and directed the opening towards the forms in the distance. Immediately, the dream world started being sucked into it.

First the distant horizon was siphoned into the bag, then the area of the middle distance, and finally the immediate dreamscape. Soon the last forms of that world were speeding towards the mouth of the bag and were gone. When all had vanished, and of this world there was left only a sensationless vacuum, the dream thief closed the bag and nodded towards Puck. Then he was gone.

Satisfied, Puck flashed back to the body which waited him in the Land of the Sad. Si-mung was awake and very excited when Puck opened his body's eyes.

"Well," Si-mung shouted, "What happened? Did you see who stole my dream?"

"I met the one who is stealing your dreams," Puck replied. "And I know what has to be done."

"You can stop my dreams being stolen?"

"Si-mung, the only being with the power to resolve this situation is you."

And Puck explained to Si-mung that he would have to travel to a far away place and there engage in certain labours. But these labours were dangerous. There was a possibility he might end up stranded in that distant place forever. Or even that he might lose his life. But unless he travelled there and carried out the required tasks, he would never resolve the dilemma of his stolen dreams.

Si-mung thought about what Puck said. He weighed the risk against his frustration. Finally, he made a decision. His eyes were shining as he turned towards Puck.

"When do we leave?" he asked.

Puck smiled. "At dawn."

Dawn came crisp and clear. And before the rest of the town was stirring, Puck and Si-mung were already far away.

Their journey took them a great distance. Across fields they walked, over mountains. Through the surging waters of rivers they forded, and along deep, stony canyons. Past villages they walked, stopping sometimes for food and drink, at other times to shelter from storms, or to sleep for a night in the comfort a straw bed. Then out into the wilderness they again trekked, evading stalking beasts and prowling men.

Finally, they reached their destination. The Sea of Desolation.

The Sea of Desolation was a small sea situated in a distant region of the Land of the Sad. In an epoch long gone, before humankind were even thought of, the Moon had been ripped out of the Earth. It had then tumbled across the skies, wailing and weeping, filling the heavens with its cries. These cries the Gods collected. They found a huge hollow in the Land of the Sad, and into this hollow they poured the collected cries. And thus it was that from the madness of the Moon the Gods created the Sea of Desolation.

Puck and Si-mung stood at the edge of the Sea's dark waters, tasting its heavy vibration. Then Puck pointed.

On the shore of the Sea of Desolation was a grove of trees. Before Si-mung was born these trees had been ancient. And they would remain long after he had gone. The grove stood in a circle, and inside this circle was a carpet of soft, green grass.

Puck led Si-mung into the grove. They sat on the grass, face to face, in its very centre. Remaining silent, they listened to the Sea's waves as they lapped the shore, felt the giant trees towering over them, and savoured the presence of this place that none of the sons and daughters of the Earth had ever before entered.

Finally, Puck spoke.

"Si-mung," he said, "we have arrived at our destination. Do you wish to solve the dilemma of your dreams disappearing?"

"I do," Si-mung replied.

"That being so, you must pass through three trials. The first trial begins tomorrow. We'll eat and sleep now. And tomorrow will bring what it will bring."

The following morning a lonely wind blew from across the waves. Although it was day, the full disc of the Moon hung over the Sea of Desolation, reminding of its past travails, stark and pale and forbidding. Standing on the cold shore, Si-mung felt naked and bereft.

"Your first task," Puck instructed him, "is to enter the waters, dive into their depths, and pluck from those depths a pearl. You will continue until you have the prize. Now, dive."

Si-mung dove.

All day he laboured, without rest. Plunging deep into the chilled waters, twisting like a seal through the currents, breaking open shell after shell in search of a pearl.

Noon came and went. The afternoon passed. And still he searched. As the light started to fade, Si-mung became frantic. Recklessly, he dived deeper and deeper. But to no avail.

Night found him dragging himself exhausted from the waters of the Sea of Desolation. And, truly, desolation filled his heart.

He staggered wearily from the shore, and entered the sacred grove where Puck was waiting. Throwing himself down, he wept.

"I've failed," he cried. "I haven't found the pearl. I'm too weak to do what you have asked. I'm sorry. I am unworthy of your help."

And Si-mung hung his head in self-disgust and despair. But Puck was smiling.

"Si-mung," he said, "you underestimate yourself. You have succeeded admirably."

Si-mung looked up at Puck through his tears.

"What do you mean?"

"The object of the first trial," Puck replied, "is to show you your inadequacy. For the truth is that you won't find the pearl entirely through your own efforts. You need the help of what is more than your self in order to achieve more than your self thinks it is capable of. By diving and not finding, and not giving up, you now know the truth of this for yourself."

Wonder passed across Si-mung's face.

"The first trial has been passed," Puck stated. "Tomorrow brings the second trial."

They ate. And soon Si-mung was sleeping soundly.

Dawn the following day found Si-mung kneeling on the shores of the Sea of Desolation. Closing his eyes, he called on those elements in the Land of the Sad that are greater than himself, that could help him achieve more than he thought himself capable of.

A long time he knelt, alternatively reaching his hands up to the sky, and bowing his head down to the ground.

The day had been still and breathless. But, by degrees, a wind stirred, blowing towards Si-mung from across the waves.

At first the wind was cold. But gradually it became warmer.

Then the wind entered Si-mung, through his mouth, through his ears and nostrils, through the pores of his skin. He felt himself being transformed into a bubble, filled by the wind.

The wind picked up Si-mung, lifted him far across the waters, then plunged him down into the waters of the Sea of Desolation. Down he was taken, down deeper than he had dived the previous day, until he reached the Sea's floor.

And there, at the bottom, surrounded by gently waving fronds of red and green seaweed, was a giant oyster. The oyster's shell was open, and within the gaping shells sat an enormous pearl radiating a beautiful, pale light.

Si-mung swam over and grasped it in both hands.

The sun was setting as Si-mung arrived at the grove, where Puck was waiting. He laid the pearl at the very centre of the circle of trees. Then he bowed and prayed, thanking the elements for their help.

When he had finished praying, he looked up and saw Puck watching him. A twinkle lit Puck's eyes as he gave Si-mung his evening meal.

"Tomorrow," Puck declared, "your task is to make the pearl disappear. Now eat and sleep."

When dawn came the following morning, Si-mung was seated in front of the pearl. It rested pure and radiant on the grass. A gentle light glowed from within it. That light touched Si-mung's face, suffusing him with calmness. He sat there and began the third task, of making the pearl disappear.

Si-mung sat thus for many hours. Sometimes he closed his eyes. Sometimes he kept them open. Sometimes he tried to will the pearl away. Sometimes he prayed to the Gods for help. Yet always, whenever he looked at it, the pearl continued to sit before him.

At first, he despaired. Then, as still nothing changed, he became indifferent. Finally, an unusual state fell on him.

He was sitting on the grass, his eyes closed, when a sensation that something was entering his body overtook him.

He opened his eyes and looked at the pearl. He then perceived what he hadn't observed before, that the pearl was really a sphere emanating light. This observation caused a feeling of joy to surge inside him. Entering this feeling, he closed his eyes. Immediately he experienced a jolt, which caused his eyes to jerk open.

Consternation followed. For Si-mung was not where he had been. He was now seated where the pearl had rested, at the very centre of the grove! He looked around, bewildered.

Puck laughed softly. "Now you are ready to dream."

The sun set in a brilliance of red and orange, rimming the clouds with a crimson glow. Below, in the grove, Puck and Si-mung ate. And when darkness settled over the Earth, they slept. Soon Si-mung was dreaming.

Si-mung dreamed of the Earth. He dreamed it was a small orb far beneath him. He wanted to escape, but there was a long string attaching him to it. He wanted to fly away into other realms and dimensions, but the string kept him tied to the Earth. It was very strong and he couldn't break it. So he began to pull.

For hours he pulled. Hours and hours.

And eventually the end came into sight. Si-mung saw that something was attached to the string's end. He pulled harder, and when the end was reached he saw ... the dream thief.

The dream thief bowed solemnly. Then he let the string loose and swooped away towards the stars, among which he vanished.

Si-mung understood what had just occurred. He was free! He clasped Puck joyously – or, at least, he would have had they each possessed bodies.

"Si-mung," Puck said, "you have broken the cord that ties you to the Earth. But know this is just a beginning. You are now free to dream greater dreams than you ever have before. May you now be dreamed by those who dispense wisdom. And may you one day dream of the Gods."

Puck bowed, then flashed away.

And Si-mung woke. He was not surprised to discover he was no longer in the grove nestled on the shores of the Sea of Desolation. Instead, he was in the room in the inn where he had originally drunk Puck's herb potion. And he was alone.

Si-mung stepped out the inn, into the street. He wrapped his cloak around his shoulders. And he strode out to realise his destiny of becoming Si-mung, Second of the Wise.

The Desert Plain

The Desert Plain lay below Puck. Devoid of life or vegetation, it consisted only of rocks, aridity, and dust. And in the middle of the Desert Plain sat Sorrow.

All day and night Sorrow wept. Her tears fell to the ground and formed a pool. That pool spread, feeding a river. And that river flowed out of the Desert Plain, into every region of the Land of the Sad.

Each inhabitant of those regions drank from that river. Many disliked its taste. Some enjoyed it too much, and went mad. But all, at some time in their lives, were drinkers thereof.

Puck smiled. And with a wave of his hand he cast his spell.

Nothing changed.

Sorrow was seated on a rocky mound.

As Puck approached her wails became louder and her features more clearly discernible. Sorrow's eyes were swollen, her face crumpled with lamentations. Her fingers wound obsessively at the trim of the quivering cloak wrapped around her shoulders.

This cloak was black, and its edges were braided with sighs. Each time she moved, the cloak was disturbed, and those sighs fell off, hovered in the air a moment, then dispersed with the sound of sadly expelled air.

Yet there was a cause for Sorrow's unhappiness. Because a group of miniature, deformed goblins, ugly, covered with diseases and blights, rolled at Sorrow's feet, shouting and arguing among themselves.

And as they fought they reached up and pulled her hair, or tweaked her flesh, or struck her body with hard, calloused hands. Thus they caused Sorrow's suffering. And therefore she wept.

Yet this was not all.

For as her tears fell, some dropped into the pool beneath her feet, contributing to the river which flowed out into the other regions of the Land of the Sad.

But other tears struck the dry dirt around Sorrow. And where they struck, they were instantly transformed into more goblins. These immediately jumped up and joined the others, punching, pricking, tormenting. So agony produced more agony. And thus was Sorrow's existence.

Puck smiled sympathetically.

"Hello, Sorrow," he said. "I wish you wouldn't weep."

Sorrow started at his voice. It was the first, besides her own, which she had ever heard.

"Who is it?" she cried. "Who tells me I shouldn't weep?"

"My name is Puck."

"Where are you, Puck? Come here and let me see you."

"I'm standing in front of you."

Sorrow looked around desperately. But her eyes were so swollen she couldn't see him. Realising this, she bowed her head and her weeping renewed.

"Don't cry," Puck said. "There's no need."

But Sorrow ignored him.

The tears fell, the sighs moaned, the goblins tormented. Yet Puck was not beaten.

Placing his hands together, Puck caught several of Sorrow's tears. He breathed on them, then threw them on the dry ground.

Where Sorrow's tears fell a lake was formed. It grew rapidly, until its sparkling blue waters stretched far away. Puck clapped his hands in satisfaction.

"Sorrow!" he called. "Look at what I have made!"

Sorrow looked at the lake. She saw how its waters sparkled and shone. A glimmer of a smile began to move through her tears. But then she saw her own face reflected in those waters. The glimmer faded, tears welled in her eyes, and her weeping intensified.

But Puck was not yet finished.

With one finger he touched the waters of the lake. Magic flickered below. And a light glowed in the depths.

And now, as each of Sorrow's tears struck the surface of the lake, it was transformed into a radiant jewel which floated on the water. Soon there were hundreds of floating jewels, all reflecting in beautiful colours the light which reached up from the depths below.

Puck gathered up some of these jewels. In his hands they formed a necklace. And Puck dropped the necklace over Sorrow's pale neck. Then he stood back and waited.

And wonderful transformation began.

Gradually, Sorrow became aware of the necklace around her throat. Slowly, her hands moved down from her face to touch the jewels. By degrees, the tears came less steadily. And, then, a miracle. Sorrow stopped weeping!

Amazed herself that such should happen, Sorrow looked up. She saw Puck standing before her, smiling.

"Come," he said, and took her hand.

She stood and allowed Puck to lead her away from her mound of rocks and along the edge of the lake.

Once again she looked down into the waters. But this time a beautiful woman looked back. Sorrow smiled. The beautiful woman, the jewels around her neck sparkling, smiled back.

"Puck!" Sorrow exclaimed joyously. "What a glory you are!"

And in her ecstasy she turned around to show the goblins what she had become. But the goblins were all gone, melted by the jewel's radiant rays.

Laughing, Sorrow ran across the Desert Plain.

And wherever her feet touched, flowers sprang up. And wherever her hands pointed, trees leaped into growth.

And Sorrow wept again, but this time in joy. And wherever her tears fell, beautiful creatures were born.

And the Desert Plain became the Fruitful Plain, where all life blossomed and came to fruition.

And Puck looked on, content.

Epilogue

Yet this was not the end of Sorrow's story. For nothing in the Land of the Sad lasts. Just so did Sorrow discover her experience to be. For Puck had cast a spell upon her. And as with every created thing, this spell had a span of time set into it. Accordingly, it could not but dissolve. And so it came to pass that Sorrow fell out of her enchantment.

Hence Sorrow descended from her state of ecstasy and glory, and returned to her normal state of being in the Desert Plain.

It inevitably occurred that Sorrow opened her eyes.

She looked around.

She saw aridity, dryness, torment. She felt the rocks beneath her, and the goblins torturing her. She raised her hands, lowered her head, and opened her heart.

And Sorrow renewed her wailing.

Sorrow's new lamentations were powerful. So powerful that they spread out across the Desert Plain.

And the winds picked them up and blew them far away, into the most distant regions of the Land of the Sad.

And there they insinuated themselves into the voices of the sons and daughters of the Earth. So whenever those people laughed, a certain bitterness echoed beneath their mirth. And many were the times in their lives when Sorrow's face was indistinguishable from their own.

But Puck's task here was ended. He rose into the air.

Leaving Sorrow in the middle of the Desert Plain, he crossed the Mountains of What Can Be, floated past the Valley of the Always Is, and looked down at the Land of the Sad, observing the sons and daughters of the Earth wherever and however they were born, lived and died.

And sometimes he interceded in their lives. And at other times he did not. And sometimes he was kind. And sometimes he was harsh. But always his actions were filled with love.

And thus Puck administers still.

To the reader

Small publishers rely on the support of readers to tell others about the books they enjoy. To support the author and *Puck of the Starways*, we ask you to consider placing a review on the site where you bought this book. Learn more about Keith Hill and his writing, including free samples, at www.keithhillauthor.com.

Attar Books has published a number of books that explore issues related to the topics explored here. If you wish to be updated on Attar Books' latest publications, join the email list at www.attarbooks.com.

Other books by Keith Hill that you may enjoy:

The Ecstasy of Cabeza de Vaca

""A tour de force. Hill's humanizing of de Vaca is the ingredient that makes it so moving and once taken up, impossible to put down." – Alistair Paterson

"An extraordinary effort of imagination. In New Zealand literature there's no one quite like Keith Hill, and certainly no long poem like this one." —Roger Horrocks

In 1528, a Spanish expedition was shipwrecked in the Gulf of Mexico. Eight years later only four men remained alive. One of the four, Cabeza de Vaca, later published an account of what occurred. Naked and enslaved, de Vaca was stripped of all he possessed, then underwent an extraordinary transformation. *The Ecstasy of Cabeza de Vaca* is Keith Hill's masterful retelling of Cabeza de Vaca's story. It is a heartbreaking account of courage and faith, barbarity and miracles, that transports us to the limits of human experience. A sample from Chapter 1 follows.

1. Landfall

We surged from the sea
ecstatic, demented
sagged on the still swaying shore
our cracked mouths filled with joy.

Five days we prayed for this
feared it would never come
that devouring death
which hovered over our swaying hopes
which filled our one sail with despair
blowing our broken raft this way, that
would feed us eventually to the deep
and all our hopes would drown there.
Now we felt firm land beneath our cheeks.
And as the tide nuzzled our beards
sucked backwards
pulled streaming sand across wrinkled hands
we raised our heads
dumbly stared into each others' eyes
and knew there was a God.
That, ultimately, all was good.

"Our Father, which are in heaven
to You we make a shameful confession:
we feared this day would never come."

Seven men we were in number
kneeled, in a circle, shoulder to shoulder
bewildered
trembling
terrified
scarce strong enough to hold ourselves erect.
Seven battered heads bowed in a rasp of prayer:

"To You who are a mystery
whose measures are unfathomable
here and now we give thanks
contented with the workings of Your will
until our time itself should end.
Through Jesus Christ, our Lord. Amen."

That "Amen" echoed in seven chastened hearts.
Then, as one, we turned our eyes
towards the land which had proved our ark.
In the darkening light of dusk
we saw a glowing stretch of sand
and a dank wall of jungle leaves.
Birds sang within, life quickening life
promising food and the luxury of shelter.
All we saw was another deep in which
who knows what terrors lurked.
No words passed that moment between us.
But, as one, we turned back towards the sea.

Man is not man without fire.
We squatted like savages

eating beach grasses
reduced as we had been by our days at sea
to that primeval state we shared
with Adam in the garden.
Except he never needed fire
being radiated by God.
And except our innocence was long lost.
I cannot speak for my emaciated men
but in my salt-wrinkled heart
and despite the savour of our prayer
I doubted we were yet saved.
All we were was not yet dead.
As we huddled together in the dark
no sleep came nor respite from our dread.
For while hard sand held our bodies firm
I could feel Leviathan sweeping the depths
that continued to sway beneath me
feeding the fear that we were abandoned
in our good God's true and just creation.

ϴ ϴ ϴ

A morning's laboured walk confirmed it.
Captain Andrés Dorantes was with me
a commonsense and courageous man
whose judgement the years had well burnished.
We tramped the lumped course of dunes
staggered where the curved shore led
often forced to stop, sit, draw deep breaths
so weak we were from our torment at sea.
Yet hours of sweat and aching stagger
but returned us to our makeshift raft:
we had beached on an island
and the jungle we had darkly feared last night

that it crawled with all palpable terrors
day revealed to be thin, straggling and safe.
No beasts threatened our survival.
We were where we had prayed to be.
Yet there was trouble in this too
for neither was there food.
The birds we disturbed by our walking
proved to be resting not feeding.
They circled the island crying
then flew out to sea.
We waited. They never did return.
Where did they fly to? Another shore?
We could but hope.
For given we would surely starve
if we made this island our final stop
that shore we knew nothing of
we had no choice but to assay.

θ θ θ

Half a day we creaked on the waves
praying wind and tide
would not pull us back to sea
too tired to row ourselves to safety
even if we knew its direction.
In truth, we were past despair
at the ocean's mercy
resigned to our God's chosen fate
when we saw a green line of tree-tops
that stood above the swelling ocean
and smoke drifting above all.
Our hearts leapt.
But hope is the cruellest emotion:
it most betrays when most heaven-sent.

For smoke meant men.
None spoke of our shared nightmare
yet each vividly knew what it was—
that we would fall in with the cannibals
we had heard the miseries of in Spain.
The most severe of this land's savages
would shatter our chests with adzes
wrest out our still throbbing hearts
throw them on the fire to roast
and suck the marrow from our bones
grinning at us all the while
we writhed our last moments of dying.
That I have written these fevered words
is witness to our unspoken fear.
That I am alive to write them now
proves how far our fear was a lie.
We lay like morsels on our fractured raft
mesmerised by knowing men
we had long prayed would find and save us
worked now not far away
feeding the fire that could finish us all.
Yet was this to be our end?
Were we too starved to save the meagre flesh
that hung now from our starkened bones?
I, Cabeza de Vaca, was not!

Other books by Keith Hill

The Bhagavad Gita: A new poetic translation

"An enthralling new rendering of a classic text that achieves the
rare feat of balancing spiritual insight, poetic power and philosophic accuracy."—Peter Calvert, author of *The Kosmic Web*

The original text is written in poetry, but it is usually rendered into English in prose. This translation balances the need to present the *Bhagavad Gita*'s profound concepts precisely while reproducing the original poem's dramatic and poetic power. Endnotes and a glossary help readers unfamiliar with Indian culture understand the poem's mythological and philosophic references.

Interpretations of Desire

"Keith Hill's artful and beautiful renditions will bring Ibn 'Arabi's neglected masterpiece to a new readership."—Nile Green, author of *Sufism: A Global History*

In 1201, the Sufi master Shaykh Muhyiddin Ibn 'Arabi arrived in Mecca, where was entranced by Nizám, the daughter of a prominent religious teacher. As Beatrice did for Dante, Nizám inspired a sequence of love poems that are Ibn 'Arabi's poetic masterpiece. This collection reveals that with his intense feeling, vivid imagery, and the playful way he reworked the conventions of Bedouin desert poetry, Ibn 'Arabi wrote poems that deserve to be placed alongside the best of his illustrious Sufi compatriots.

Psalms of Exile and Return

"Refreshes the meaning of ancient works while relating age-old struggles to the present day. Much here to consider and enjoy."—Raewyn Alexander, *Magazine*

In 587 BCE, King Zedekiah of Judah led his people in rebellion against Babylonian rule. Nebuchadnezzar responded mercilessly. His army sacked Jerusalem, destroyed the Temple, and deported thousands to Babylon. These sequence of psalms are written from the perspective of one of those exiles, recounting his growing despair in Babylon, his escape and reuniting with his lost beloved, and their return to Jerusalem.

Out of the Way World Here Comes Humanity!

"Up-to-the-minute reportage on our fraught zeitgeist, conveyed with vitality and satirical humour." —Hugh Major, author of The Lantern in the Skull

Written by a fed up boomer determined to call out our collective stupidity, *Out of the Way World* is simultaneously unblinkingly realistic, cavalier and funny. Themes include Covid, climate change, biodiversity loss, the Anthropocene, politicians, conspiracies, work, America, trolls and the future. The humour is as disturbing as it is engaging.

The God Revolution

Best Book: Ashton Wylie Book Awards 2011

"Deserves to be read by all those who care about ideas, the trajectory of civilization and its future form." — Peter Dornauf, www.eyecontact.com

"Hill's exposition is a fine example of scrupulously rigorous scholarship—it is remarkable how much ground is covered within his brief historical survey. In addition, he discusses a wide range of academically abstruse subjects in consistently lucid, nontechnical prose." —Kirkus Review

All these books may be purchased at your favourite online store or ordered through your favourite bookshop. To read chapter excerpts and find out more about them go to attarbooks.com.

www.ingramcontent.com/pod-product-compliance
Lightning Source LLC
Chambersburg PA
CBHW030754110726
47900CB00008B/2593